Fliss's whole body felt hot now, hot and alive, and pulsing with need.

When his hips brushed against hers, she felt an urgent desire to push herself against him. But what would she do if she discovered he was as aroused as she was? She had no experience in playing the seductress.

In any case, it would never happen, she assured herself grimly. Whatever game he was playing, he would never let it go that far. Teasing her, tempting her, that was his objective. He wanted her to know what she was missing in her life. As if she didn't know that already…

New York Times bestselling author **Anne Mather** has written since she was seven, but it was only when her first child was born that she fulfilled her dream of becoming a writer. Her first book, CAROLINE, appeared in 1966. It met with immediate success, and since then Anne has written more than 140 novels, reaching a readership which spans the world.

Born and raised in the north of England, Anne still makes her home there with her husband, two children, and now grandchildren. Asked if she finds writing a lonely occupation, she replies that her characters always keep her company. In fact, she is so busy sorting out their lives that she often doesn't have time for her own! An avid reader herself, she devours everything from sagas and romances to mainstream fiction and suspense. Anne has also written a number of mainstream novels, with DANGEROUS TEMPTATION, her most recent title, published by MIRA® Books.

Recent titles by the same author:

THE FORBIDDEN MISTRESS

SAVAGE AWAKENING

BY
ANNE MATHER

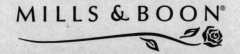

MILLS & BOON®

First published in Great Britain 2005
Harlequin Mills & Boon Limited,
Eton House, 18-24 Paradise Road, Richmond, Surrey TW9 1SR

© Anne Mather 2005

ISBN 0 263 84128 6

Set in Times Roman 10 on 11 pt.
01-0305-58278

Printed and bound in Spain
by Litografía Rosés, S.A., Barcelona

CHAPTER ONE

IT WAS the chimes of the church clock that woke him.

Ironically enough, he'd grown used to sleeping through the wailing call of the muezzin. Four years in North Africa, the last eighteen months in an Abuqaran jail, had made such sounds familiar to him. That, and the staccato shots that erupted from time to time across the prison yard.

Not that he'd slept well, of course. A thin blanket thrown on a concrete floor was hardly conducive to a sound—let alone a comfortable—slumber. But it was amazing what the body could get used to, how little sustenance it needed to survive.

Still, he had survived, and after six months back in England he should have become accustomed to the ordinary sounds of civilised living again.

But he hadn't. He was still coming to terms with the fact that he was not the man he used to be and whether or not he slept well—or at all—was a small problem in the larger scheme of things.

Not liking the direction his thoughts were taking, he thrust back the covers and swung his legs out of bed. At least sitting up no longer caused the sickening feeling of dizziness he'd suffered during his first few weeks of freedom. And his limbs, which had been almost skeletal when he returned, were gradually filling out, his muscles strengthening with the regular workouts he subjected himself to every day. The doctors had warned him not to try and do too much, but there'd been no way he could control the desire to regain his health and strength, and moving at a steady pace had never been good enough for him.

Consequently, although his psychological problems showed

little sign of improvement, physically he felt much better than he had even a month ago.

Which was such a sucker, he chided himself grimly, pressing down on the mattress and getting a little unsteadily to his feet. Sometimes he had the feeling he'd never make it, never recover even the belief in himself he'd once enjoyed. Perhaps it would be kinder all round if other people realised it, too.

Nevertheless, he'd had to give it a try. And, to that end, he'd bought this house in a village far enough from London and the life he and Diane had had there before he'd been sent to Abuqara to cover the civil war.

Diane didn't approve of his decision. Mallon's End was the village where she'd grown up and where her parents still lived. She thought he was crazy wanting to leave the exciting opportunities London presented behind. He'd already been offered his old job with a commercial television station back again and she couldn't understand why he'd turned it down. He didn't honestly know himself. But, thanks to the legacy his grandmother had left him, money wasn't a problem, and there was always that offer of a book deal if he should choose to write about his experiences as a prisoner of the rebel forces in Abuqara.

He crossed the floor to the windows, shivering a little in the cooler air. The polished boards beneath his feet were cold, too, but he didn't notice them. He was used to going barefoot. The first thing his captors had done was take his shoes away from him. And although initially his feet had blistered and been agony to walk on, gradually they'd hardened up.

All the same, he was used to temperatures that usually hovered near forty degrees Celsius in daylight hours, and although England was supposed to be enjoying a heatwave at the moment, he hadn't noticed.

Pulling the curtain aside, he peered out. Outside the long windows, the gardens of the house stretched in all directions, lush with colour. To someone used to bare walls or stark packed-earth streets stripped of any sign of civilisation, it was an amazing view. Even the months he'd spent since his return in his comfortable apartment in Belsize Park hadn't prepared him for so much beauty. This was what he needed, he told himself, what he'd dreamed of while he was in prison. It was a humanising experience.

Beyond the grounds of the house, the churchyard offered its own kind of absolution. He could see cottages through the swaying branches of the elms and yews that guarded the lych-gate, and an occasional car passing the bottom of his drive on its way into the village proper.

It was all so—yes, that word again—civilised. But he was still isolated from the people and places that had once been so familiar to him. It was strange but while he was a prisoner, he'd longed for company, for someone who spoke his own language.

He'd had some conversations with the captain of the rebel forces. Fortunately, he'd known a little of his language, and the man had been surprisingly intelligent and well read.

Yet now he was home, he found himself shunning company, avoiding conversation. He was a mess, he thought ruefully. Diane was right. He wouldn't blame her if she got sick of trying to get through to him.

Even so, he thought as he moved away from the windows, given the hassle of the last few months, surely he had a right to some peace, some tranquillity. God knew he hadn't been prepared for the amount of interest his return had engendered, but what with interviews, phone-ins, online question-and-answer sessions, he'd begun to feel persecuted all over again. He'd wanted out, not just out of London, but out of that way of life. His old way of life, he acknowledged. And if that meant he was cuckoo, then so be it.

A shower removed a few more of the cobwebs that were clouding his system, and after towelling himself dry, he dressed in drawstring sweat pants and a black cotton T-shirt. He pulled a rueful face at his roughening jawline and decided he liked not having to use a hair-dryer. In North Africa his head had been shaved, and since his return he'd kept his hair barely long enough to cover his scalp. Diane said it suited him, but then, she'd say anything to boost his self-esteem. She was worried about him, worried about their relationship. And he couldn't say he blamed her.

The house felt chilly as he went downstairs. It was barely seven o'clock, after all, and until he'd worked out how the central heating operated, he'd have to live with it.

But at least the place had central heating, he mused gratefully. These old houses often didn't, but the previous owner had apparently demanded that comfort and he was glad.

Nevertheless, he would have to see about getting some decorating done. The heavy flock wallpaper on the stairs and the crimson damask in the main reception room would definitely have to go, and he needed a lot more furniture than the bed and the couple of armchairs he'd brought with him. The rest of his furniture was still in his London apartment and, until he'd definitely decided he was going to stay here, it would be staying there.

But this place was big enough for several living and bedroom suites and he couldn't exist with what he had. He would have to visit a saleroom; an auction saleroom, perhaps. These rooms would not take kindly to modern furniture.

Thankfully, the kitchen faced east and already it was warm and bathed in sunlight. Like the rest of the house, it could do with some updating, but he decided he rather liked the rich mahogany units and the dark green porcelain of the Aga.

However, the Aga presented another problem and, rather than try to figure it out this morning, he started a pot of coffee filtering through the strong Brazilian grains he preferred and turned with some relief to the gas hob.

Pretty soon, the kitchen was filled with the appetising scents of hot coffee and frying bacon and he was glad his mother had suggested taking a box of groceries with him. Left to himself, he would probably have had to go out for breakfast and that was definitely not part of his plan.

The kitchen windows overlooked the gardens at the back of the property and he stood staring out at an overgrown vegetable plot as he drank his first cup of coffee of the day. There was such a lot to do, he reflected with a twinge of apprehension. Had he bitten off more than he could chew?

But, no. The whole idea was that he should be able to fill his days to the exclusion of all else. He didn't want time to relax, time to think. Until he'd figured out whether he was ever going to feel normal again, simple manual labour was what he needed.

The sound of footsteps clattering across the paved patio outside brought his brows together in a frown. Dammit, he thought. No one was supposed to know he was here yet. He'd deliberately stowed the four-by-four in the garage to disguise his presence. Who the hell had discovered he'd moved in?

He moved closer to the windows and looked out. He couldn't see anyone and that bothered him, too. He had heard the footsteps, hadn't he? He couldn't be starting having hallucinations. God, that would be the last straw!

He drew back, setting his coffee down on the pine-blocked table behind him. But as he moved to check on the bacon, he heard the footsteps again and a sick feeling of apprehension invaded his stomach.

There was no one there. He would have seen a shadow cross the window if anyone had really walked past. Which meant? Which meant *what?*

Swearing, he moved to the door and, flicking the lock, he yanked it open, all in one fluid motion. And disturbed a young girl who was squatting down beside what looked like a rabbit hutch, feeding dandelion leaves into the cage.

He must have frightened her, he thought, his own feelings of relief flooding his system with adrenalin. But it was good to know he wasn't losing his mind as well as his—

He severed that thought and forced a rueful smile to his lips as the girl got hurriedly to her feet. Sufficient unto the day, he quoted grimly. He was alive, wasn't he? And sane? Which was definitely a bonus.

'Who are you?'

The words caught him unawares. That was his question, he thought, half resenting her presence of mind. She was looking at him as if he was the intruder, and he gave a rueful shake of his head.

'My name's Quinn,' he said, humouring her. 'Who are you?'

'Um—Nancy,' she answered, after a moment. 'Nancy—Drew.' And then, before he could comment on her name, a frown creased her childish features. 'Do you live here?'

'I do now,' said Quinn drily. 'Is that a problem?'

Nancy shrugged. 'No,' she conceded, but she sounded less sure of herself now. 'That is—you don't have a dog, do you?'

Quinn grinned. He couldn't help himself. 'Not at present,' he replied, considering it. 'Do you like dogs?'

'I do.' Nancy sounded doubtful none the less. 'Grandad has a dog. A retriever. But he's very naughty.'

'Who, your grandad?'

Quinn couldn't help himself and Nancy gave him a reproving look. 'No!' she exclaimed impatiently. 'Harvey. He used to chase Buttons all around the garden. He was terrified!'

'Harvey?' asked Quinn innocently and Nancy's face took on a suspicious stare.

'Buttons,' she corrected him. 'You're teasing me, aren't you?'

Quinn sighed. 'Just a little.' He paused. 'Who's Buttons?'

'My rabbit,' said Nancy, squatting down again and pointing to what Quinn now saw was a cage, as he'd thought. 'Mummy said I ought to find another home for him. So I did.'

Quinn suspected her mother had not meant in someone else's garden, but he didn't say anything. Instead, he hunkered down beside her and saw the white nose of what appeared to be quite a large rabbit nuzzling at the wires of its cage.

'This is Buttons,' went on Nancy, performing the introduction. 'Isn't he sweet?'

'I guess.' Quinn knew nothing about rabbits so his opinion was limited. 'But isn't his cage rather small?'

'Mmm,' Nancy agreed. 'That's why I used to let him out. But as I said—'

'Harvey chased him,' Quinn finished for her and Nancy nodded.

'He doesn't realise that Buttons is frightened of him.'

'Well, dogs chase rabbits,' said Quinn matter-of-factly. 'It's what they do.'

'So—can he stay here?' asked Nancy quickly, and Quinn got abruptly to his feet.

'I—maybe,' he said slowly. 'If your mother approves.'

'Oh, she doesn't know,' said Nancy airily, standing up, too. Then, more anxiously, 'You won't tell her, will you?'

Fliss had opened her mouth to shout Amy's name again when she saw her. The door to the Old Coaching House was open and a man was standing on the threshold talking to her daughter.

A relieved breath escaped her. She hadn't really been worried, she assured herself, but you heard such awful stories these days about children being abducted and Amy was only nine years old.

Nevertheless, she didn't approve of her coming here without permission, even if Amy was naturally familiar with the place. She'd accompanied her mother often enough during school holidays and the like and she knew the grounds almost as well as her own garden.

But that didn't alter the fact that things had changed now. Old Colonel Phillips was dead and, although she hadn't heard about it, the Old Coaching House had apparently been sold. To someone Amy didn't know, Fliss reminded herself, quickening her step. How many times had she warned her daughter not to talk to strange men?

The man became aware of her presence before her daughter did. His head turned and she got a swift impression of a hard, uncompromising face with dark, deeply tanned features. He was tall, that much was obvious, but there didn't appear to be an ounce of spare flesh on his leanly muscled frame.

He looked—dangerous, she thought fancifully, not liking the conclusion at all. He looked nothing like the people who usually retired to Mallon's End, and she wondered why someone like him would choose to buy a house in such a quiet, unexciting place.

She got the distinct impression that he would have preferred to cut short his conversation with Amy and close the door before she reached them. But something, an unwilling acceptance of his responsibilities—or common decency, perhaps—persuaded him to at least acknowledge her before he made his escape.

For her part, Fliss was more curious than anything else. As she got nearer, she could see that he was younger than she'd imagined; possibly late thirties, she guessed, with very short dark hair that added to his harsh appearance.

But for someone who looked so menacing, he was absurdly attractive. Goodness! Fliss swallowed a little nervously, feeling butterflies fluttering in her stomach. Who on earth was he?

'I—I'm sorry,' she began, deciding an apology was in order. 'If my daughter's been troubling you—'

'She hasn't,' he said, his voice low and a little hoarse, and Fliss saw the way Amy's shoulders hunched in the way she had when her mother embarrassed her.

'Oh, Mum!' She grimaced, casting an impatient look in Fliss's direction. 'I'm not a baby, you know.'

Fliss reserved judgement on that one. In her opinion Amy was still young enough to warrant the anxiety she had felt at her disappearance.

'I've been looking for you,' she said, deciding any chastisement could wait until later. 'Didn't you hear me calling you?'

Amy shrugged now. 'I might have done,' she said airily, but Fliss wondered if it was only her imagination that made her think her daughter was looking slightly uneasy now. What had been going on, for heaven's sake? What had this man been saying to her?

'Well, why didn't you answer, then?' she demanded, before allowing their audience a slight smile. 'I was worried.'

'I'm sure Nancy didn't mean to cause you any unnecessary distress, Mrs Drew,' the man broke in abruptly, and if Fliss hadn't been so shocked by the name he'd used, she'd have

realised there was an increasing weariness in his harsh tone.
'No harm done.'

'You think not?' Fliss couldn't let it go. She looked down
at her daughter. 'Amy? Did you tell this—gentleman—that
your name is Nancy Drew?'

Amy flushed now. 'What if I did?'

Fliss shook her head. 'I don't believe it.'

The man breathed heavily. 'I gather that's not her name?'

'No.' Fliss tried to control her temper. It wasn't his fault,
after all. 'It's Amy. Amy Taylor. Nancy Drew is just—'

'Yeah, I know who Nancy Drew is.' He interrupted her drily.
'Way to go, Nancy. Solved any exciting cases lately?'

Amy pursed her lips, but she reserved her anger for her
mother. 'Now see what you've done!' she exclaimed. 'You've
made me look silly in front of Quinn!'

'Quinn?'

Fliss's eyes moved to the man again and glimpsed the spasm
of resignation that crossed his face. 'Matthew Quinn,' he
agreed flatly. 'I've bought this place.'

'Oh.' Fliss wondered why he seemed so reluctant to tell her
that. 'Oh, well—good,' she murmured. 'I hope you and your—
er—family will be very happy here.'

'I don't have a family,' he replied in that harsh, abrasive
voice that Fliss found as sexy as his appearance. 'But thanks.'

'You're welcome.'

Fliss managed a polite smile and then caught her lower lip
between her teeth. Would this be a good time to explain why
Amy felt she had a right to enter his garden at will? Maybe he
would need a housekeeper, too. If he didn't have a wife...

'Come on, Mum.' Amy caught her arm now and attempted
to pull her away. 'It's nearly time for school.'

'Is it?'

Fliss's brows narrowed. Since when had Amy been so eager
to go to school? Her suspicions resurfaced. What had she been
doing? What had this man been saying to her that she didn't
want her mother to know about?

Her eyes returned to his dark face, but when he met her gaze with a cool appraisal she was forced to look away. Her gaze dropped down over his tight-fitting T-shirt, over drawstring sweat pants that couldn't hide the impressive bulge of his sex, the powerful length of his legs. And bare feet. Her skin prickled. He must have just got out of bed.

Had Amy awakened him?

And then she saw the box-like structure that was wedged beside the doorstep and comprehension dawned. The compulsive—if unwilling—awareness his hard male beauty had had on her disappeared beneath a sudden wave of frustration.

Grasping Amy's arm before she could get away from her, she pointed to the offending item. 'What is Buttons's hutch doing here?' she demanded shortly. 'Is he inside?' She dipped her head. 'Yes, I can see he is. Come on, Amy. What is he doing here?'

Amy's shoulders drooped and Fliss wasn't at all surprised when her eyes moved appealingly to Matthew Quinn. Of course, she thought irritably. He must have known about this. That was what he and Amy had been talking about when she'd interrupted them. And he hadn't said a word, even though he must have realised that she hadn't been aware of what was going on.

She turned on him then, prepared to voice her indignation—however unjustified that indignation might be—and found him leaning tiredly against the frame of the door. His face was drawn now and scored with a haunting weariness she was sure wasn't just the result of lack of sleep.

Immediately, all thought of reprimanding him fled. The man looked ill, for goodness' sake. And exhausted. Or utterly bored by their exchange.

'Um—are you all right?' she ventured, and at her words he seemed to make a conscious effort to recover himself.

'A little fatigued is all,' he assured her firmly, but he backed into the kitchen as he spoke and now she could smell the acrid aroma of charred bacon. He glanced behind him, evidently noticing the same problem, and, forestalling any offer she might have made, he added, 'Can we continue this at some other time, Mrs Taylor? I'm afraid my breakfast is burning.'

CHAPTER TWO

FLISS endeavoured not to think about Matthew Quinn again until she'd taken her daughter to school.

Instead, she'd concentrated on Amy's behaviour, on how disappointed she was that the little girl had lied to her. When, faced with the prospect of Buttons being sent to the local animal shelter for his own safety, Amy had come up with a solution of her own, her mother had been relieved. A friend at school had offered the rabbit a home, she'd said, and Fliss had allowed her to take Buttons away on her grandfather's wheelbarrow, never dreaming that Amy had had no intention of giving the rabbit to anyone.

Now, however, her deception had been discovered, and in the most embarrassing way possible. Matthew Quinn either considered Fliss was an unfit mother—a label that had been slung at her more times than she cared to remember since, at the age of sixteen, she'd discovered she was pregnant—or an unfeeling one, which was probably worse.

Amy, attempting to justify her actions, had assured her mother that 'Quinn' hadn't minded the fact that he had had an unwanted squatter on his land, but Fliss believed she knew better. From what she'd seen of him, she thought Matthew Quinn was not a well man, and he'd probably only been humouring the child to avoid further argument.

Whatever, Fliss was faced with the not-very-pleasant task of returning to the big house to collect the rabbit and make her apologies. Again. Amy wouldn't be pleased, particularly if she was once again forced to consider the prospect of Buttons living out his days at the animal shelter, but it couldn't be helped. Whatever Matthew Quinn had said, she doubted he would re-

15

ally appreciate having a furry mammal—however appealing—
on his premises on a permanent basis.

And if he did have a wife…

Just because he'd said he didn't have a family didn't nec-
essarily mean…

But that was one speculation too far. Fliss had no intention
of making that mistake. OK, he was one of the most attractive
men she'd ever seen. He was also one of the most dangerous
to her peace of mind and, with or without a wife, he was way
out of her league.

Her father was up by the time she got back from taking Amy
to school.

Until four years ago George Taylor had run the small pharmacy in the village. But a dwindling population—due to the
shortage of jobs, and many houses being bought as second
homes by city-dwellers—plus the cheaper attractions of the supermarket in nearby Westerbury, had hastened his retirement.
These days he supplemented their income by writing articles
for the local paper, occasionally babysitting Amy when Fliss
worked occasional evenings at the local pub.

Harvey, her father's retriever, barked and jumped up at her
excitedly when she let herself into the cottage, and she wished
the dog would act his age. Harvey was seven years old, for
heaven's sake. Old enough to behave himself. But he still acted
like a puppy and her father spoiled him outrageously.

'Everything OK?' he asked now as Fliss came into the
kitchen, where he was enjoying his breakfast of toast and marmalade, and she dropped down into the chair opposite him and
pulled a face.

'As it will ever be, I suppose,' she grumbled, reaching for
the coffee pot and pouring herself a cup. 'I've just discovered
where Buttons is living.'

'The rabbit?' Her father put his paper aside and regarded his
daughter curiously.

'Yes, the rabbit.' Fliss scowled.

'Well, I thought Amy had found him a home,' he said, puzzled. 'Don't tell me she's keeping the rabbit in her room.'

'No. Nothing like that.' Fliss shook her head. 'She's been keeping it at the Old Coaching House.'

Her father started to laugh and then subdued it. 'Well, the little monkey,' he said instead. 'Still, it doesn't matter, does it? The place is empty.'

'As a matter of fact, it's not,' declared Fliss, taking a sip of her coffee. 'There's a new tenant. Or rather, a new owner. I met him this morning.'

'Really?' George Taylor looked surprised. 'They've kept that quiet. I didn't even know it was on the market.'

'Nor did I.' Fliss looked momentarily wistful. 'It certainly brings it home to me that Colonel Phillips is gone for good.'

'Hmm.' Her father nodded, and then reached across the table to pat his daughter's hand. 'He was very old, Fliss. What was he? Ninety-two or -three?'

'Ninety-one,' said Fliss firmly. 'And I know he was old. But he was very kind to me.'

Her father sighed. 'And you were kind to him, too. I doubt if he'd have got anyone else to do all his housework as you did.'

'He paid me,' Fliss protested. 'I miss that income, I really do.'

'Well, I can't say I'm sorry you're not working as a domestic any longer,' declared her father, buttering another slice of toast. 'You deserve better than that. I don't know what your mother would say about you wasting your degree.'

Fliss sighed now. This was an old argument and one she didn't particularly want to get into today. It was true, while her mother was alive, she had been able to leave Amy with her and attend the local university. But when her mother died in a car crash just a year after she'd graduated, she'd had to give up her job as a trainee physiotherapist to look after Amy herself.

There'd been no question of paying a child minder. Her father's business had been folding and money was scarce. And, although he'd offered to babysit, he'd had enough to do coping with his own grief. Looking after a lively four-year-old would have been too much for him to manage.

Now, of course, he could have coped, but Fliss didn't think it was fair to ask him. He'd settled happily into his retirement and he would have missed being able to go to the library when he felt like it, calling in at the pub for a drink, gossiping with his cronies.

'Anyway, we weren't talking about me,' she said, taking another swallow of coffee. 'Hmm, this is good. Why does my coffee never taste like this?'

'Because you don't put enough coffee in the filter,' replied her father comfortably, slipping a crust of bread beneath the table for Harvey to take. Then, seeing his daughter's eyes upon him, he added swiftly, 'Anyway, maybe the new owner will want a housekeeper, too.'

Fliss knew he'd never have said that in the ordinary way. It was just to divert her from his persistent habit of feeding the dog at the table, and she pulled a wry face.

'I don't think so.'

He frowned now. 'Why not?' He paused. 'Oh, perhaps they already have a housekeeper, hmm?'

'Perhaps they do.' Fliss felt curiously loath to discuss Matthew Quinn with her father. 'In any case, I'm going to have to go over there and fetch the rabbit back.'

'Do you want me to do it?'

It was tempting, but Fliss shook her head. She wanted—no, needed—to see Matthew Quinn again. She needed to explain why Amy had felt free to deposit the rabbit on his doorstep.

When Colonel Phillips was alive and Fliss had worked at the house three mornings a week, Amy had often accompanied her. The old man had been especially fond of the little girl and he'd encouraged Fliss to bring her along. So, whenever Amy had been away from school, for holidays and suchlike, she'd been a welcome visitor at the house.

Sometimes the colonel had played board games with her, and she'd been fascinated by his display cases filled with coins gleaned from almost a century of collecting. The house had been an Aladdin's cave to the little girl, and she'd been encouraged to share it.

In consequence, Amy had missed him almost as much as Fliss when he'd suddenly been taken into hospital. She hadn't understood why she couldn't go to visit him and, although Fliss had explained the circumstances of his illness, she suspected the child still regarded the Old Coaching House as his home.

When he died the house had been inherited by a distant cousin, who had apparently lost no time in putting it on the market, Fliss thought wryly. No one in the village had known anything about it or she was sure her father would have picked up the news on the grapevine.

Now she got up from the table, carrying her empty cup across to the sink. The overgrown lawn at the back of the cottage reminded her that she had other jobs she'd promised herself she'd do today. Dammit, if only Amy had let the rabbit go to the shelter and been done with it.

'So what's the new owner like?' asked her father, getting up from the table to bring his own dishes to be washed. Then he opened the door to let the dog out, stepping outside for a moment and taking a deep breath of the warm, flower-scented air. 'Mmm, those roses have never smelt better,' he added. 'I don't know why you don't bring some of them into the house.'

Because I don't have the time, thought Fliss grimly, fighting a brief spurt of irritation. But it would never have occurred to her father to do something like that himself. No more than it occurred to him to wash his own dishes or make his own bed in the mornings. She filled the washing-up bowl with soapy water and dropped his cup, saucer and plate into the hot suds. She sighed. She mustn't let her annoyance over the rabbit influence her attitude towards her father. He was the way he was, and there was nothing she could do about it.

But despite his admiration for the roses, he hadn't forgotten his original question. 'Who is he?' he asked, coming back into the kitchen. 'The man you spoke to at the big house? Did he tell you his name?'

Deciding there was no point in prevaricating, Fliss shrugged.

'I think he said his name was Quinn,' she replied carelessly. She finished drying the dishes and hung the tea towel over the rail to dry. 'I might as well go and get Buttons now. You never know, he may have gone out. Do you think it would be all right if I took the rabbit without his say-so?'

'Why not?' asked her father, but he was looking pensive. 'Quinn,' he said ruminatively. 'Quinn.' He frowned. 'Where have I heard that name before?'

'The Mighty Quinn?' suggested Fliss, giving her reflection a quick once-over in the mirror beside the hall door.

She looked unusually flushed, she thought ruefully, and she hadn't even set out on her mission yet. Pale skin, that never tanned no matter how long she stayed out in the sun, had the hectic blush of colour, vying with the vivid tangle of her hair. Blue eyes—her father insisted they were violet—stared back with a mixture of excitement and apprehension, and she felt a frustrated surge of impatience. She wasn't going on a date! She was going to rescue a rabbit, for pity's sake.

'I know!' Her father's sudden exclamation had her swinging round in surprise to find him balling a fist into his palm. 'That name, Quinn. I knew I'd heard it recently. That's the name of that man—that journalist—who spent about eighteen months as a prisoner of the rebels in Abuqara. You remember, don't you? They did a documentary about it on television recently. He escaped. Yes, that's right, he escaped. But not before he'd suffered God knows what treatment at the enemy's hands.'

Fliss swallowed with difficulty. Her breath suddenly seemed constricted somewhere down in her throat. 'I—don't remember,' she said faintly.

But she did. Now that her father had reminded her of it, she remembered the documentary very well. Not that Matthew Quinn himself had appeared in it. It had simply been an examination of the situation in Abuqara, with Matthew Quinn's imprisonment used to illustrate the violence meted out to foreigners who got caught up in the country's civil war.

'Not that I'm suggesting that your Mr Quinn is the same man,' her father was going on, unaware of his daughter's reaction. 'That would be a bit of a coincidence, don't you think? What with his aversion to the media and me being a part-time hack myself.'

'Y-e-s.' Fliss let the word string out, not sure why she didn't just admit what she was thinking there and then. But the memory of Matthew Quinn's dark, haunted face was still sharply etched in her mind, and, if he was who she thought he was, she couldn't betray him. Not even to her own father. 'Um—I ought to get going. I'll take the car. I can easily dump the hutch in the back.'

'Right.' But her father was still looking thoughtful and her nerves tightened. 'Perhaps I ought to come with you. Introduce myself, welcome him to the village, show him we're a friendly lot. What do you think?'

'I—no.' Fliss realised he might take umbrage at the sharpness of her tone and hurried to justify herself. 'I mean—I don't think this is a good time, Dad. What with the trouble over the rabbit and all. Let's let the dust settle, hmm? We don't want—the family—to think we're pushy.'

'Well, you could be right.' He looked downcast. 'It's a pity, though. It would have been a good opportunity to get to know them.'

'Later,' said Fliss fervently, picking up the car keys. 'See you soon.'

'Wait.' As she was about to leave, her father came after her. 'How are you going to lift the hutch into the car? It's heavy, you know. It was all Amy could do to push it on the wheelbarrow.'

'I'll manage.' Fliss thought she'd do anything rather than have her father discover who the new occupant of the Old Coaching House was because of her. As he'd said, he took his journalism seriously, and he wouldn't be able to resist talking about a scoop like this. 'Bye.'

It was only a few minutes' drive from the cottage to the Old Coaching House. Their cottage adjoined the grounds of the church on one side and the Old Coaching House adjoined them on the other.

But there the similarity ended. Cherry Tree Cottage was set in a modest garden whereas the Old Coaching House had extensive grounds, with lawns and flowerbeds and an apple orchard, as well as a tennis court at the back of the house.

As she drove, Fliss had to concede that Amy had done well to wheel the rabbit this far. Of course, when Fliss was working for Colonel Phillips, they had taken the short cut around the back of the church, but it was still some distance. She gave a rueful smile. Amy had obviously been determined to keep the pet that one of her school friends had given her.

The front of the old house was still impressive, despite its air of faded grandeur. Stone gateposts, with rusting iron gates that hung rather optimistically from them, gave access to a drive that definitely required some maintenance. Fliss's father's elderly hatchback bumped rather resentfully over the holes in the tarmac, and Fliss realised she would have to make sure the rabbit hutch didn't bounce out again as she was driving home.

Tall poplars lined the drive, framing the house with greenery. The rhododendron bushes that flanked them had been a mass of colour a couple of weeks ago, but now they were shedding their brilliant petals onto the grass verge. They made Fliss feel sad. Colonel Phillips had loved those rhododendrons.

There was a car parked at the foot of the shallow steps that led up to the terrace, one of those expensive off-roaders, much favoured by people who wanted to make a statement about their financial status. It was not the sort of car Fliss would have expected Matthew Quinn to drive—if he was the Matthew Quinn her father had been talking about—but what did she know? She was a humble single mother who had to serve bar meals and clean other people's houses just to make ends meet.

And how pathetic did that sound?

Parking the Ford beside the BMW, Fliss turned off the engine and opened her door. Sliding her legs out of the car, she wished she'd taken the time to change before coming back. Her sleeveless vest and canvas shorts were all very well for taking Amy to school, but they hardly created an impression of responsible motherhood. But then, she reflected, if she had changed, her father might have wondered why and that might have opened another can of worms.

Taking a deep breath, she rounded the car and mounted the steps to the heavy oak door. She couldn't help noticing that no one had polished the brass work recently, or swept the terrace, and she pulled a wry face. It was true. She was developing a servant's mentality. Go figure!

Dismissing such thoughts, she lifted the knocker and let it fall, wincing as it echoed around the building. There was no way anyone could ignore that.

There was silence for a few moments and Fliss was just considering knocking again, when she heard the sound of footsteps crossing the hall. They didn't sound like a man's footsteps, however, and she steeled herself for the ordeal of identifying herself to Matthew Quinn's wife. She just hoped he'd clued her in to what had happened. She was going to feel such a fool if he hadn't.

She straightened her spine, drawing herself up to the full five feet six inches she'd been blessed with. Squaring her shoulders, she looped back several strands of bright coppery hair behind her ears. As if that would improve her appearance, she thought wryly. She looked what she was; a slightly harassed woman in her mid-twenties, with a little too much weight both above and below her waist.

'I'm sorry to disturb you—' she was beginning as the door opened, and then broke off in surprise. 'Diane,' she exclaimed, recognising the girl she had used to go to school with. 'Diane Chesney!' She hesitated as the obvious thought struck her. 'Or should I say *Mrs* Quinn?'

'Diane will do,' retorted the other woman shortly. She arched an enquiring brow. 'Can I help you—Felicity, is it?'

Great!

Fliss blew out a breath. It was obvious that whatever the circumstances of Diane's being here, she had no desire to rekindle old friendships. Fliss couldn't believe she'd forgotten how much she hated her name, or that there was any doubt about her identity.

But it was also obvious that her—husband? Boyfriend? Whatever—had conveniently forgotten to mention the uninvited visitors he had had earlier.

'Well…' She murmured now, feeling even more inadequate in the face of Diane's cool sophistication. 'I've come to get my daughter's rabbit.'

'Your daughter's rabbit!'

Clearly Diane had no idea what she was talking about. Her contemptuous tone proved it and, unwillingly, a memory surfaced of Diane using that tone to her before. It was when Fliss had first confessed to her friend that she was going to have a baby. She'd been seeking advice, understanding. But all Diane had done was urge her to have an abortion.

'You're too young to have a sprog!' she'd exclaimed scornfully. 'Do yourself a favour, Fliss. Get rid of it. I would.'

With hindsight, Fliss had to admit that Diane had had a point. She had been too young, too innocent, too infatuated with the boy who had taken advantage of her to know exactly what she wanted to do. She'd been afraid to tell her parents; scared of what they might say; desperate for a way out.

In the event, it was her mother who had come to her rescue. Lucy Taylor hadn't thought twice. Fliss should have the baby, she'd said. She'd help her. Both her parents would help her. They'd also supported her decision to have nothing more to do with the father of the child. Terry Matheson had denied everything, of course, and thankfully he'd left the district long before Amy was born.

Nevertheless, Fliss's pregnancy had driven a wedge between her and Diane. She'd had to postpone taking her higher-level exams for a year and, by then, Diane had moved on.

They could have resumed their friendship, of course, but Diane hadn't been interested. She was having too good a time at university in London to care about a girl who, in her opinion, had as good as ruined her life.

By the time Diane graduated, her parents were telling everyone that she was an art expert, that she was going to be running a gallery in the smartest part of town. The fact that she rarely visited her parents was always conveniently forgotten. Diane was soooo in demand; soooo busy. They were soooo proud of her.

And now, here she was, apparently living with the man who, either with or without his consent, had become a minor celebrity in his own right.

No surprise there, then.

'Amy's rabbit,' Fliss continued, trying not to let the other woman's attitude faze her. 'I spoke to your—er—?'

'My fiancé?' suggested Diane condescendingly, and Fliss nodded.

'I guess,' she said. She moistened her lips. 'I gather he didn't mention it.'

'Why would he?' Diane rolled her eyes. 'I'm sorry, Fliss, but Matt and I have more important things to talk about than a bloody rabbit, for God's sake!'

So she did remember her name, thought Fliss smugly. But Diane was annoyed about something. That was obvious. And it was evidently nothing to do with her and Amy.

'OK.'

Fliss was trying to decide how to explain the situation in the briefest terms possible when Matthew Quinn himself appeared behind Diane. He was still barefoot, Fliss noticed unwillingly, his expression only marginally less hostile than his fiancée's.

'What's going on?' he asked impatiently, and then he saw Fliss. 'Oh—Mrs Taylor.'

Diane snorted at this and he paused a moment to give her a curious look. Then, with a shrug, he went on, 'Did you want something else?'

Fliss's cheeks had flushed at Diane's scornful reaction to her name, but she refused to be daunted. 'It's Miss Taylor, actually,' she said, telling herself she didn't care what he thought of her. 'I've come to collect the rabbit.'

'Ah.' Matthew Quinn glanced again at the woman beside him. He frowned. 'Forgive me, but do you two know one another?'

'We used to.' Diane answered him before Fliss could say a word. 'But we lost touch many years ago.'

Matthew's only response was a sudden arching of his brows, but Fliss had no intention of continuing this. 'Is it all right if I back the car along the path beside the house?' she asked. 'Then I can just lift the hutch into the boot.'

'What's all this about?' demanded Diane, clearly not liking the idea that Fliss and her fiancé had some unfinished business she didn't know about. 'Where is this rabbit, for heaven's sake? And what's it doing here?'

'It's a long story,' said Matthew carelessly. Then, to Fliss, 'You don't have to move it, you know.'

'Oh, I think I do,' she retorted stiffly. She turned away. 'I'll get the car.'

By the time she'd reversed the Fiesta along the service lane, he was waiting for her. Still barefoot, he had hoisted the rabbit's cage into his arms, and when she hurriedly got out to lift the hatch, he shoved the hutch inside.

'Thanks,' she said, a little breathlessly, noticing that he seemed out of breath, too. 'I'm sorry.'

'No problem,' he assured her, leaning forward with his hands on his thighs, taking a few gulping breaths of air. 'God, I'm out of condition. I guess I need to get myself in shape in more ways than one.'

Fliss forced a faint smile. 'I think you need to rest,' she murmured carefully. Then, glimpsing Diane watching them from the corner of the house, 'Thanks again. I'll try and keep Amy out of your hair in future.'

CHAPTER THREE

DIANE was pacing about the kitchen when Matt came back inside. 'D'you want to tell me what's going on?' she demanded, her grey eyes flaring with irritation. 'How long have you and Fliss Taylor known one another?'

Matt gave her an incredulous look. 'We don't know one another,' he said, going to wash his hands at the sink. 'How the hell would we? I've only been here a couple of days.'

'You tell me.' Diane was huffy. 'You seemed pretty familiar with one another. And she obviously didn't expect to see me. Didn't you tell her I was coming down this morning?'

'Oh, for pity's sake!' Matt dried his hands and then shoved them into his pockets so she wouldn't see they were shaking. 'Why would I tell her anything? I've only met her once before.'

Diane regarded him suspiciously. 'So what was that rabbit doing here?'

Matt heaved a sigh. He badly wanted to sit down, but dogged determination—and pride—kept him on his feet. He should have known Diane would come here looking for trouble, but however appealing Fliss Taylor might be—and he couldn't deny she was appealing—he wasn't interested.

'She has a kid,' he said wearily. 'But then, you probably know that. You're the one who seems to know everything about her.'

'I used to,' declared Diane dismissively. 'Personally, I haven't set eyes on her or her kid for years.'

'OK.' Matt endeavoured to control his irritation. 'Well, for some reason, the kid decided her rabbit would be safer in my garden than hers. She'd stowed its cage near the back door and I caught her feeding it this morning. That's all there is to it.'

'So—then what? You phoned her mother and asked her to come and get it?'

'No.' Matt was tired of this interrogation. He didn't know why Diane had bothered to come if all she intended to do was pick an argument with him. Surely she knew he was supposed to avoid any unnecessary stress, and getting riled up about something so trivial was definitely unnecessary. He blew out a breath. 'She came here looking for her daughter. No law against that, is there?'

Diane's lips tightened. 'I suppose not.'

'Good. I'm glad we agree on something, at any rate.' Matt turned away. 'Want some coffee?'

'So why didn't they just take the rabbit with them?' she asked after a moment, and Matt swore.

'For pity's sake,' he snapped. 'Does it matter? I've explained what happened. Let that be an end of it.'

Diane hesitated. 'I—suppose it would have been difficult to move the thing without a car.'

'Right.'

Diane nodded. 'And Fliss didn't know the kid had left the rabbit here?'

'Diane…'

Matt's tone warned her not to proceed, but she spread her hands defensively. 'I just want to know,' she said innocently. 'I suppose Amy still regards this place as her second home.'

Matt swung round then, a frown drawing his brows together. 'What are you talking about?'

Diane looked smug now. 'I thought you were sick of talking about it,' she mocked, and then, realising she was pushing her luck, she gave in. 'Fliss used to work for the old man who owned this place,' she explained. 'I've heard she used to bring the kid with her.'

'What work did she do?'

'What do drop-outs usually do?' asked Diane contemptuously. 'She was his housekeeper, of course. When she wasn't working in the pub, that is.'

Matt poured coffee into two mugs and handed one to her.

'For someone who claims not to have seen the woman for God knows how long, you seem to know a lot about her,' he said, sinking gratefully onto one of the two stools he'd brought down from London. He swallowed a mouthful of coffee, feeling the reassuring kick of caffeine invading his system. 'Are you a snob, Diane?'

'No!' She was indignant. 'But I can't help it if I think she was a fool to throw away a decent education to be a single mother.'

Matt arched a dark brow. 'Is that what she did?'

'Yes.' Diane scowled. 'I mean, she was sixteen, for God's sake. She must have been crazy.'

'Obviously she didn't think so.'

Diane shrugged. 'More fool her.' She shook her head. 'It was the talk of the village.'

'I bet.'

'Well, it was so stupid. She could have had an abortion. No one need have known anything about it. It wasn't as if the boy wanted to marry her. Mummy thinks her mother never really got over it.'

'Ah.' Matt was beginning to understand. 'So you get your information from your mother.'

Diane looked offended. 'There's no need to take that attitude. Mummy thought I'd be interested. After all, Fliss and I used to be friends.' She grimaced. 'To think, I used to be like her!'

Matt was not prepared to get into that one. Instead, he concentrated on his coffee, knowing that sooner or later Diane would remember what they'd been talking about before the other woman had knocked at the door.

And he didn't have to wait long.

'Anyway,' she said, 'that doesn't matter now. You were telling me what you intend to do with this place. I mean, look around you, darling. It's going to take a fortune to make it anything like habitable.'

'A small fortune, perhaps,' he allowed, with a wry smile. 'And I don't intend to do it all at once. Just the main bedroom and a couple of reception rooms. Most of the changes are cosmetic, anyway. According to Joe Francis, the building's sound enough.'

'But what does it matter?' protested Diane, setting down her mug with hardly controlled frustration. 'Matt, you're not going to stay here. You may kid yourself that this is what you want, but that's just a passing phase. As soon as you're feeling yourself again, you'll realise that you can't live anywhere but London. Your job's there; your friends are there. You don't know anyone in Mallon's End. Except Mummy and Daddy, of course, and you don't really care for them. Admit it.'

'I know Mrs—*Miss* Taylor,' remarked Matt, knowing it would annoy her. But dammit, she was annoying him right now. 'And you don't know what I want, Diane. What you're talking about is what *you* want. How do you know my priorities haven't changed?'

'Because I *do* know you!' she exclaimed fiercely. 'You'll soon get bored doing nothing. Even if you don't need the money.'

Matt shrugged. 'We'll see.'

'Oh!' Diane's exclamation was impatient. 'All right, what about me? Have you thought about me at all? I can't live here. My job's in London.'

'I know that.'

'And?'

Matt bent his head, rubbing palms that were suddenly slick with sweat over the knees of his pants. 'And—I think it would be a good idea if we cooled it for a while—'

'No!'

'Yes.' Matt knew he was being harsh but he really didn't have a choice. Not in the circumstances. 'Help me on this, Diane. I need some time on my own; time to get my head straight.' He paused, considering his words. 'Pretending things are the way they used to be isn't going to do it.'

'It could.' Diane quickly crossed the room to kneel at his feet. 'Darling, don't do this to me. To us. We're so good together.'

We were, thought Matt flatly, making no attempt to touch her. 'Diane—'

'No, listen to me.' She looked up at him appealingly, her heart-shaped face alight with enthusiasm, grey eyes entreating now, eager to persuade him she was right. 'I can help you, darling. You know I can. But not if you send me away.'

'Dammit, I'm not sending you away,' he muttered grimly, but she wasn't listening to him.

Moving his hands aside, she replaced them with her own. For a moment, she was still. And then, watching him with an almost avid concentration, she slid her hands along his thighs to the apex of his legs. Her intention was clear. When she licked her lips, he could see her anticipation. Then, she spread his legs and came between them...

Matt couldn't let her go on. With a surge of revulsion, he thrust her aside and sprang to his feet. Somehow he managed to put the width of the room between them, his pulse racing, his heart hammering wildly in his chest. But it wasn't a good feeling. He felt sick, and sickened, by what she'd tried to do, and he could hardly bear to look at her now.

'Well...' Diane got to her feet, bitterness and disappointment etched sharply on her flushed face. 'You had only to say no, Matt. There was no need to practically knock me over in your eagerness to get away from me.'

Matt groaned. 'Diane, please—'

'At least I know where I stand,' she went on, patting down her skirt, brushing a thread of cotton from the silk jersey. 'What happened in Abuqara, Matt? Did you suddenly acquire a taste for different flesh from mine? Or was it something even more extreme? A change of sex, perhaps?'

Matt's hands balled into fists at his sides. 'I think you'd better go, Diane,' he said harshly. 'Before I forget I was brought up to be a gentleman.'

She stared at him for a moment, and then her face crumpled, the coldness in her expression giving way to a woeful defeat. 'Oh, Matt,' she breathed, scrubbing at the tears that were now pouring down her cheeks, 'you know I didn't mean that. I love you. I'd never do anything—*say* anything to hurt you.'

Matt felt weariness envelop him. It was all too much. Diane was too much. She had no idea how he was feeling and he didn't have the urge—or the patience—to deal with her histrionics.

That was why he'd bought this house in the first place. He'd known Diane would not be able to accompany him and he'd persuaded himself that she'd come to see it was the best solution for both of them. He still cared about her, of course he did. But she had to understand that his attitude had changed, his aspirations had changed. He was not the man he used to be.

God help him!

'Look,' he said at last, crossing his arms against any attempt she might make to touch him again, 'I know this has been hard for you, Diane. It's been hard for both of us. And I don't expect you to give up your life in London and move down here.'

Diane sniffed. 'So what? You're giving me the brush-off.'

'No.' Matt gave an inward groan. 'I'm not saying I never want to see you again—'

'Is that supposed to reassure me?' Diane pushed back her silvery cap of hair with a restless hand. 'Matt, I thought you loved me; I thought that one day we might—well, you know, make it legal.'

'And I'm not saying we won't. One day,' said Matt steadily. 'Come on, Diane, you know I'm right. It's just not working right now.'

Diane regarded him from beneath her lashes. 'And that's all it is? This—need you have for some time alone, for some space?'

'I swear it.' Matt spread his hands. 'What do you think? That there's someone else? Goddammit, Diane, when have I had the chance to find someone else?'

'I don't know everything you did while you were in Abuqara,' she protested. 'Tony said that Abuqaran women are really beautiful—'

'Tony!' Matt was scathing. 'I might have known Tony Corbett had a hand in this. Since when has he been such an expert on Abuqaran women?'

Diane shrugged a little defensively now. 'He was only speaking objectively.'

'I'll bet.'

Diane pulled a face. 'He's my boss. He cares about me.' She paused. 'I'm glad he's wrong.'

'Yeah.' Matt managed a faint smile in response. 'So—what are you going to do? I'd offer to let you stay the night but only one of the rooms is furnished.'

'We could always share—' began Diane, and then cut herself off with a wry grimace. 'No, scrub that. I can't stay in any case. I've got a meeting with the board of governors this afternoon and I've promised to have dinner with Helen Wyatt this evening. She's hopefully going to give the gallery some good publicity and I wouldn't want to disappoint her. No, I'll drop in on Mummy and Daddy and then I'll head back to town. I suppose I just wanted to assure myself that the move had gone OK, to assure myself that you were all right.' She paused. 'And obviously you are.'

Matt inclined his head. 'Thanks.'

Diane managed a bright smile. 'My pleasure,' she said, restricting herself to a quick squeeze of his arm. 'OK, you look after yourself, right? I'll be in touch again in a couple of days.'

The words 'I'll look forward to it' stuck in Matt's throat and he gave a rueful smile instead. 'You take care,' he said, as she picked up her handbag and headed towards the front door.

'I will,' she replied, and he felt guilty when he heard the sudden break in her voice. 'Bye.'

''Bye,' he answered roughly. But he closed his eyes against the sudden surge of relief he felt as the BMW crunched away down the drive.

'I've been thinking, perhaps I could build a run for Amy's rabbit in the garden. That way, Harvey wouldn't be able to chase him. What do you think?'

It was a couple of days later and Fliss was making a shopping list to take to the supermarket in Westerbury when her father joined her. He had spent most of the morning editing an article he was writing about the need for care in the community, but now he came to lean on the table next to her chair.

Fliss looked up in some confusion. In all honesty, although her fingers were busy detailing the household goods and foodstuffs they needed, her mind had been far away. Well, across the churchyard actually, she conceded drily. Despite her resistance, Matthew Quinn had had that effect on her.

'I'm sorry,' she said, blinking rapidly. 'What did you say?'

'The rabbit,' said her father patiently. 'I was wondering whether it would be a good idea for me to build it an enclosure in the garden.'

'Oh.' Fliss endeavoured to get her brain in gear. She hesitated. 'Do you think you could?'

'I dare say.' He straightened and regarded the expanse of lawn beyond the windows. 'We can't keep the poor thing trapped in its hutch all day, can we?'

'I suppose not.' Fliss shrugged. 'Unless I take Buttons to the animal shelter while Amy's at school.'

'You wouldn't do that,' said her father firmly. 'OK. I think there are some slats of wood in the shed. Perhaps you could get me a roll of netting when you go into Westerbury. A couple of metres should be enough.'

'More than enough,' agreed Fliss drily, hoping he wouldn't destroy her flowerbeds in the process. She got to her feet. 'What shall we have for lunch?'

It was a quarter to two when Fliss parked the Fiesta on the lot adjoining a small retail park. A do-it-yourself outlet, an electrical store, an auction warehouse—where Fliss sometimes liked to browse—and a supermarket circled the central parking area. Fliss liked its location because it was situated at the edge of town. It meant she didn't have to negotiate the maze of one-way streets that characterised the central part of the city.

It was hot, the grey spire of the cathedral rising tall and impressive against the vivid blue of the sky. She knew she was lucky to live in this part of the country. It was very busy at this time of year, of course, with foreign tourists and more local traffic thronging the streets and clogging up the main arteries. But it was worth it for the times when there were no visitors, and she could walk along Cathedral Close and visit the ancient church without being jostled by the crowds.

She had got what she needed from the supermarket and was stowing her shopping in the car when she saw him. He was coming out of the auction warehouse and, judging by the fact that the manager had accompanied him outside, she guessed he'd bought something substantial.

Or maybe Harry Gilchrist had recognised him. Fliss knew the man who was with him. Harry Gilchrist's son was in the same class as Amy at the village school. A single father himself, he'd often tried to draw Fliss into conversation. He evidently thought they had a lot in common, but Fliss didn't encourage single men. Or married men, for that matter, she thought wryly. She was happy the way she was.

Now, however, she wished she had been a little more friendly. Then she might have felt free to saunter across the car park and exchange a few words with him and Matthew Quinn. Just to find out what Quinn had been buying, she assured herself firmly. Not with any idea of presuming on what had been a very brief acquaintance.

In any case, Diane was probably with him, she thought. Just because she wasn't visible at the moment didn't mean she wasn't around. It was the most natural thing in the world that a couple who were planning on setting up home together should look for suitable furniture. Yet, knowing what she did of Diane, Fliss wouldn't have expected her to want old—albeit valuable—furnishings.

Still…

She turned back to the car and finished packing her shopping into the boot. It meant wedging things together, but she didn't want a jumble of spilled goods when she got home. Then, closing the hatch, she straightened—and looked directly into Matthew Quinn's eyes, staring at her from across the car park.

For a moment she was immobilised by his gaze, which seemed more penetrating than the brilliance of the sun beating down on her bare head. Had he recognised her? Was that why he was staring at her? What was she supposed to do about it? Smile? Wave? Ignore him? What?

The dilemma was taken out of her hands when he nodded in her direction. Yes, she thought, feeling the erratic quickening of her heartbeat, he had recognised her. She felt ridiculously gratified that in spite of Diane's hostility he did remember who she was. But then, it had only been a couple of days since he'd seen her. And he had been a journalist, after all.

She'd confirmed his identity by following her father's example, when he was researching a story for his column, and checked the Internet. And, although the pictures they'd shown of him didn't compare to the way he looked now, she'd been left in no doubt that he was the same man. He'd been gaunt-featured and skeletally thin when he'd returned from his imprisonment in Abuqara, but the strength of character and intelligence in his face had been unmistakable.

She hadn't told her father who he was, however. She'd consoled herself with the thought that it wasn't her job to expose the fact that they had a celebrity living in their midst. It was bound to come out sooner or later. Maybe Harry Gilchrist would be the one to blow his cover. Just so long as it wasn't her. For some reason, that was important.

Deciding that the netting her father had asked her to get could wait, Fliss pulled her keys out of her pocket and started towards the driver's door. It had suddenly occurred to her that she hadn't bothered to change before she came out. In a white cotton vest and pink dungarees that fairly screamed their chain-store origins she'd be no match for Diane in her expensive designer gear. She wasn't a vain woman, but she had her pride. She had no desire to allow the other girl to embarrass her again.

She swung open the car door, but before she could get inside, she heard someone call her name. Matthew Quinn was striding across the tarmac towards her and there was no way she could pretend she hadn't noticed him.

Once again, she was impaled by the distracting intensity of his gaze, and she found herself turning to press her back against the car, holding on to the handle of the door with nervous fingers.

'Mr Quinn,' she said, clearing her throat as her voice betrayed her. But in narrow-fitting chinos and a black T-shirt, he made her nerves tingle, his dark eyes and hard features more familiar than they should have been. 'How—how are you?'

'I'm getting there,' he said drily, regarding her so closely she was sure no aspect of her appearance had gone unremarked. 'How about you? How's—what's its name—Buttons getting on?'

'Oh—he's OK.' Fliss wondered if anyone would believe they were standing here having a conversation about a rabbit. She swallowed, forcing herself to look beyond him. 'Is Diane with you?'

'No.' He didn't elaborate. 'Are you heading home now?'

'Yes.' Fliss lifted her shoulders awkwardly. 'You don't need a lift, do you?'

'Would you have given me one?' he enquired, a trace of humour in his voice, and Fliss felt her cheeks heat at the deliberate *double entendre*.

'Of course,' she replied, refusing to let him see he'd disconcerted her. 'Well, if you don't need my help...' She glanced behind her. 'I suppose I'd better be going...'

'Do you have time for a coffee?'

If she'd been disconcerted before, his question caught her totally unawares and she gazed at him with troubled eyes. 'A coffee?'

'Yeah.' His mouth turned down. 'You know, an aromatic beverage beloved of our so-called civilised society?'

'I know what coffee is,' she said a little stiffly.

'Well, then...?'

Fliss hesitated. She was getting the distinct impression that he was already regretting the invitation, but he'd made it now and he'd stand by it.

So why shouldn't she take advantage of it?

'All right,' she said, feeling a little *frisson* of excitement in the pit of her stomach. 'Where do you want to go?'

Matthew Quinn frowned. 'Well, there's a coffee shop in the supermarket, isn't there? Or—' His mouth thinned. 'We could go back to my place.'

'The supermarket sounds fine,' said Fliss hastily, turning to lock the car again. She moistened her lips. 'If you're sure.'

'Why shouldn't I be sure?' he demanded, and then sudden comprehension brought a sardonic twist to his mouth. 'Oh, right. You think I might want to avoid public places, yeah?'

Fliss gave a nervous shrug. 'It's your call.'

'But you know who I am, right?' he persisted, and she gave him a defensive look.

'Did you think I wouldn't?'

'Perhaps I hoped,' he admitted, moving closer as another car came to take the slot beside Fliss's. 'I guess the whole village is twittering about it.'

'You flatter yourself!'

Fliss used the retort to put some space between them. The other car had initiated an intimacy she hadn't expected and she couldn't deny she was flustered. The brush of his arm against hers had stirred an awareness that pooled like liquid fire in her belly and she was desperate to escape before he realised she was unsettled by his nearness.

'Do I?' he asked now, falling into step beside her as she hurried towards the supermarket. 'How's that?'

'Well, I didn't say anything!' exclaimed Fliss hotly, feeling an unwelcome trickle of perspiration between her breasts. Rushing about in this heat wasn't just unwise, it was stupid. 'If you don't believe me—'

'Did I say I didn't believe you?' he countered softly. Then hard fingers fastened about her upper arm, bringing her to an abrupt stop. 'OK, let's start again, shall we? I know I probably seem paranoid to you and I'm sorry. It's what comes of spending the last six months trying to pretend I'm normal. Obviously I'm not being very successful.'

Fliss's eyes widened. 'Don't be silly,' she said after a moment. 'Of course you're normal. It's me. I'm too easily offended. But, honestly, I haven't told anyone who you are.'

His lips twitched. 'I believe you.'

'Good.' Fliss forced a smile, even though she doubted anything he said would slow her pulse. 'So—do you want to go in?'

Matthew Quinn smiled then, which did nothing for her rattled equilibrium. Yet there was a vulnerability about that smile—as well as a raw sensuality—that seemed to tug almost painfully at her heart.

The fact that he'd actually said nothing to warrant such a reaction disturbed her quite a bit. She had no reason to feel sorry for him, for heaven's sake. Or was feeling sorry for him her defence? The alternative—that she might be attracted to him—was definitely a more dangerous proposition.

'You wouldn't reconsider my offer of coffee at my house,' he said at last, when she was almost at breaking point. 'Maybe you're right; maybe I do flatter myself. But right now, I've got no desire to risk being stared at yet again.'

CHAPTER FOUR

HE WAS sure she would refuse.

As he released her arm and stepped back from her, he realised he was banking on it. He'd already regretted issuing the invitation, however urgent his motives had been. All he really wanted to do was go home and close his door against the world. He wasn't up to entertaining anyone. Diane's visit had proved that. So what in hell was he doing inviting this young woman back to his home and risking his fragile independence yet again?

She was looking at him now, her blue eyes wide and troubled. What was she thinking? he wondered. That she couldn't trust him? That he was some crazy nutcase who was suffering a bad attack of paranoia? If so, she was probably right.

She looked so innocent, he thought irritably. Which couldn't be true. What had Diane said? That she'd got herself pregnant at sixteen? Hardly the behaviour of an innocent. And women could effect any number of disguises. Diane had proved that, too.

But this girl was nothing like Diane. He knew that. For one thing, Diane would never go out without make-up, or give so little regard to her appearance. OK, Fliss Taylor's skin was smooth and creamy and seemed to need little improvement, but her hair clashed wildly with the pink overalls she was wearing, and, judging by the way her breasts moved, she wasn't wearing a bra beneath that skimpy T-shirt—

Hold it! Where the hell had that come from? It was a long time since he'd even noticed a woman's breasts.

'All right,' she said suddenly, startling him out of his guilty reverie. 'Let's do that.' Was it only his imagination or was she putting a brave front on it, too? 'I assume you came in your own vehicle.'

Matt's gaze moved automatically to where he had parked the Land Cruiser. 'Oh—yeah,' he said, his heart sinking. He was going to have to go through with this. 'D'you want me to follow you home or vice versa?'

'I'll follow you,' she said at once, and he wished he hadn't given her the option. Now he was going to be aware of her behind him, watching his every move, all the way back to Mallon's End.

Great!

'OK,' he said now, forcing a polite smile. 'I'll get going.'

In fact it wasn't as bad as he'd anticipated. She kept a comfortable distance between them the whole way and he'd already parked the Toyota and got out of the driving seat before she turned up the drive.

Fortunately Matt had visited the supermarket himself before he'd accosted her and now he hauled a couple of plastic carriers out of the back of his vehicle before wrestling his key into the lock.

'Come on in,' he said, backing up against the door to allow her to precede him into the hall. 'You'll have to forgive the state of the place. I haven't gotten around to doing any decorating yet.'

'Actually, I like it the way it is,' she said as he closed the door behind them, and he remembered why he had wanted to talk to her in the first place.

'Yeah, right,' he said, edging past her when she paused to look up the curving staircase. 'Diane said you used to work here. Is that true?'

A faint colour invaded her creamy cheeks as he spoke. 'I might have done,' she said, and he sensed she wasn't as comfortable with it as Diane had implied. Her steps definitely slowed as she reached the kitchen. 'Where is Diane, anyway? Did she suggest I might be interested in working for you? Is that what this is all about?'

He dumped the carriers on the pine table before he looked

at her again. 'Diane's in London,' he said flatly. 'I'm sorry if you expected she'd be here. I'm afraid there's only me.'

Fliss's soft lips pressed together for a moment. 'But she did suggest that I might be glad of a job, didn't she?' She gave a rueful shake of her head. 'I should have known.'

Matt hesitated only a moment. 'If you know Diane at all then you should know that she'd never suggest I employed any woman under the age of fifty. Especially not someone she seems to regard as a rival.'

He heard her suck in a breath. 'You're joking, right?'

He hadn't been, but Matt regretted being so honest. 'Yeah, maybe,' he said, knowing Diane would definitely not approve of him saying that. 'Anyway, forget it. Which do you prefer? Tea or coffee? I have both.'

She hesitated. 'Um—tea would be nice,' she said at last. 'Do you need any help?'

Matt's mouth compressed. 'Why? Do I look as if I do?' He plugged in the kettle. 'No, don't answer that. My ego's not up to it at the moment.'

A trace of humour touched her lips. 'I'm sure that's not true either.' She wrapped her arms about her midriff. 'What did Diane tell you about me?'

Matt didn't want to get into that. 'Not a lot,' he said, not altogether truthfully. He unloaded some steak and a couple of pre-cooked meals into the fridge. 'I guess Amy's at school right now, isn't she?'

Fliss nodded. 'She's in year five at the village primary. You must have seen the school as you drove through.' She paused and then went on. 'So—do you need a housekeeper?'

Matt was taken aback. He wasn't used to people speaking their minds so openly. Since his return, the opposite had been true. Even his mother verbally tiptoed about him, as if she wasn't entirely sure what he might do if she said the wrong thing. But Fliss Taylor…

'I—I need some help around the house,' he agreed neutrally.

'And when Diane told you I used to work for Colonel Phillips, you thought *snap!* She can work for me, too.'

Matt abandoned the rest of the shopping and propped his hip against one of the mahogany units. 'It wasn't quite like that.'

'But that is why you approached me in the car park,' she persisted, and he gave a concessionary shrug.

'All right. I admit, I thought about it.'

Her brows drew together. 'But now you've changed your mind?'

'No! Yes!' Matt heard the kettle boiling and turned gratefully to make the tea. He sighed. 'You make it sound as if I could have no other reason for speaking to you. We're not exactly strangers, for pity's sake. I mean, I made no complaint about your daughter dumping her rabbit on my doorstep, did I?'

'Gee, thanks.'

Her sardonic response was hardly unexpected and he turned to face her again with weary compliance. 'OK,' he said. 'That was uncalled-for. You both thought the house was empty. I know that. But, just for the record, when I first came out of the showroom and saw you across the car park, the idea of asking you to work for me was far from my mind.'

And that was true, he conceded, half amused by the admission. But with the sun adding gold lights to the coppery beauty of her hair, she'd been instantly recognisable. And, although the prospect of offering her a job had given him a reason to speak to her, he might have done so anyway.

Or not.

Her sudden decision to leave the doorway and cross the room towards him disrupted his thought processes. For a crazy moment, he wondered if something in his face had given her the impression that he was attracted to her and he moved almost automatically out of her way.

He realised his mistake when she cast him a pitying glance and reached instead for the two mugs he'd filled with hot water. With casual expertise, she spooned the two used tea bags into the waste bin and then said drily, 'I don't like strong tea. Do you?'

Matt felt furious with himself as he shook his head. For heaven's sake, he was doing everything he could to reinforce the opinion she probably already had of him. Cursing under his breath, he opened the fridge and pulled out a carton of milk. He set it down on the counter beside her rather more heavily than was wise and predictably some spilled onto the marble surface. He swore again. 'Sorry.'

Fliss added milk to both cups. Then, cradling hers between her palms, she said softly, 'Did I do something wrong?'

Matt felt a wave of weariness envelop him again. 'No,' he said flatly. 'It's not you. It's me. Like I said before, I'm not finding it easy to—to interact with people.'

Fliss frowned. 'Is that why you've moved out of London?' she asked, and then coloured. 'Oh, sorry. It's nothing to do with me.'

'No.' He conceded the point. 'But it's the truth.' He picked up his own cup and swallowed a mouthful of tea. 'I needed some space. London offers very little of that.'

She absorbed this, her eyes on the beige liquid in her cup, and, against his will, he noticed how long her lashes were. For someone with red hair, they were unusually dark, too, but lighter at the tips, as if bleached by the sun.

His jaw tightened. As if it mattered to him. She could be a raving beauty, with a figure to die for, and he wouldn't be interested. He wondered what she'd say if he told her that.

'I suppose Diane's parents said this house was for sale,' she ventured now, and Matt accepted that she deserved some explanation.

'No,' he assured her. 'As you might have guessed, Diane isn't in favour of me moving out of London. I found the house on a property website. It sounded exactly what I was looking for so I bought it.'

'Sight unseen?' She was obviously surprised.

'Well, I had Joe Francis, an architect friend of mine, look at it,' he said, a little defensively. 'And I did speak to the Chesneys. They seemed to think it was OK.'

'And what do you think, now that you've moved in?'

'I like it.' He smiled in spite of himself. 'I'll like it better, of course, when it feels less like a mausoleum and more like a home.'

Fliss glanced about her. 'Colonel Phillips didn't think it was a mausoleum.'

'No, well, he probably kept the place furnished.' He paused, wondering how much he should tell her. 'That's what I was doing in Westerbury. Buying some furniture that won't look out of place in these rooms.'

'From Harry Gilchrist,' she said, and Matt quirked an eyebrow.

'You know him?'

'He lives in the village,' she said regretfully. 'I suppose he recognised you.'

Matt finished his tea and set his empty mug down on the counter. 'Did he ever,' he said, pulling a wry face. 'Oh, well, I guess a week is better than nothing.'

'You might be surprised.' Fliss finished her own tea and, to his surprise, moved to the sink to wash up the cups. 'Most of the villagers tend to mind their own business.'

'Do they?'

Matt spoke almost absently, his eyes unwillingly drawn to the vulnerable curve of her nape. She'd tugged her hair to one side and secured it with a tortoiseshell clip, and the slender start of her spine was exposed.

He wasn't thinking, or he would have looked away, but instead his eyes moved down over the crossed braces of her dungarees. A narrow waist dipped in above the provocative swell of her bottom, the loose trousers only hinting at the lushness of her hips and thighs. Her legs were longer then he'd imagined, her ankles trim below the cuffs of her trousers.

'What do you mean?'

Her words arrested whatever insane visions he had been having, and he shook his head as if that would clear his brain. For

God's sake, what was he doing? And what was she talking about? He was damned if he could remember.

'I beg your pardon?'

His apology was automatic, but her expression as she turned towards him fairly simmered with resentment. 'You said, *Do they?*' she reminded him tightly. 'What did you mean?'

Matt didn't know whether to feel relieved or disappointed. For a moment there, he'd been entertaining himself with the thought that he was just the same as any other man. Of course, he wasn't, but she didn't know that. And she probably thought he was leering at her like any other member of his sex.

'You know,' she said flatly, as he struggled to answer her, 'when you said Diane hadn't told you a lot about me, you were lying, weren't you? Have the decency to admit it.'

'You're wrong.' Matt blew out a breath. 'Whatever I said, it had nothing to do with anything Diane had said about you. But, OK, she didn't tell me that you were still at school when you got pregnant. However, that has nothing to do with me.'

'Damn right.'

There was a catch in her voice now, and Matt silently cursed Diane for getting him into this. 'Right,' he said, folding his arms across his chest. 'So, shall we put that behind us and start again?'

'Whatever.' She finished drying the cups and moved towards the door. 'I'd better be going. Amy will be home from school now and she's quite a handful for my father.'

'I'll bet.' He kept his mind firmly on what she was saying and not on the curling strands of red-gold hair that had escaped the clip and were bobbing beside her cheek. He chewed at the inside of his cheek for a moment, relishing the pain as a distraction. 'You—er—you wouldn't still consider working for me, I suppose?'

She halted, but she kept her back to him as she spoke. 'Doing what, exactly?'

Matt knew an almost overwhelming urge to touch her then. She suddenly seemed so vulnerable, so alone. Which was ridiculous really, considering she had a father and a daughter who probably thought the world of her. Yet he sensed that he'd hurt her and he didn't know how to repair the damage.

He thought about asking what she used to do for Colonel Phillips, but that would sound as if he was being flippant and he couldn't have that. Instead, he prevaricated. 'Whatever needs doing,' he said. 'I won't expect you to do anything I wouldn't do myself.' He paused. 'I guess what I need is help, that's all. Just a few days a week if that suits you.'

Fliss shrugged. 'I can do that,' she said. Then she half turned, looking at him over one creamy shoulder. 'With one proviso.'

'Which is?'

'I won't work for you when Diane comes to live here,' she said. 'This is only a temporary arrangement—'

'Diane won't be coming to live here,' he broke in impulsively, and he saw the look of disbelief that crossed her face.

'But she's your fiancée!'

'She's my—what?' Matt stared at her. 'She told you that?'

'Yes.' She looked uncertain. 'She is, isn't she?'

Matt allowed a sound of frustration to escape him, realising he couldn't deny they had had a relationship. 'We—she and I—we have been involved, yeah,' he admitted unwillingly.

A faint smile touched her lips. 'I thought so,' she said, and he had to stifle the urge to explain that the situation—his situation—had changed.

'That still doesn't alter the fact that she's not going to be living here,' he said instead, more forcefully than was necessary. 'Diane's a city person. She works in London. It wouldn't be feasible for her to move down here.'

Fliss held up her hand as if to stop him. 'Not immediately, I understand that—'

'Not at all,' he said flatly, and knew he was being far too obdurate. He took a deep breath. 'What do you think?'

'I think that's your business—'

'I mean, about the job,' he said grimly, not altogether sure she wasn't mocking him, and she shrugged.

'When would you want me to start?'

Matt's initial reaction was to say, *How does tomorrow suit you?* But tomorrow was Saturday and he doubted she'd want to start then.

'Would Monday be OK?' he asked. 'Your friend, Gilchrist, is delivering the furniture I ordered on Monday morning. I'd be glad of your help.'

'All right.' She pushed her hands into the pockets of her dungarees. 'I'll come over about nine, does that suit you?'

'That's great,' he said, and as she moved out into the hall he followed her. 'See you Monday, then.'

'Monday,' she agreed, opening the door before he could get past her and do it for her. 'G'bye.'

Matt waited until she'd turned her car and driven away before he closed the door and sagged back against it. He felt exhausted and he didn't honestly know why. It wasn't as if she'd said or done anything to deplete his energies and yet he felt drained. And strangely let down, which was something new for him.

Straightening, he made his way back to the kitchen and surveyed the room with frustrated eyes. What was wrong with him now, for God's sake? He'd just completed a satisfactory shopping trip and found himself a part-time housekeeper into the bargain. What more did he want?

A hell of a lot more, he conceded grimly, but it wasn't going to happen. Nevertheless, for a short time there he'd found himself having thoughts he hadn't had since he'd got back from North Africa. He didn't kid himself it meant anything. Despite what his doctors had said, he knew he was never going to be the man he was. But Fliss Taylor was different. She intrigued him. And, like anyone else, he responded to that.

He knew he'd never met a female who was as unaware of herself as she was. There was no artifice about her, no desire to draw attention to herself, no overt sexuality. Yet she was all woman, with a soft innocence that any man would have found challenging.

Any man but him, that was, he reminded himself, the reason for his sense of dissatisfaction no longer so obscure. He picked up one of the mugs they had used and flung it across the room, uncaring when it shattered against the Aga. He had to keep reminding himself he was only half a man, he taunted himself savagely. And if that was true, what the hell was he doing hiring a housekeeper who aroused any kind of feelings inside him?

CHAPTER FIVE

'I'VE got another job.'

Fliss made the announcement as her father came into the kitchen to have his breakfast on Saturday morning. She'd intended to tell him the previous afternoon, but Amy had been home and it would have been difficult to have a private word with him then. Well, that was her excuse, anyway.

Now, however, Amy had had her breakfast and had gone out into the garden with Harvey. The child and the golden retriever were racing round the lawn at present, chasing a ball that Amy was trying to play with and generally tearing the place up. Fliss decided she would have to have a word with Amy later. She was getting too old to act so irresponsibly.

Her father took a seat at the table as Fliss set a pot of coffee and a rack of toast in front of him, and then said stiffly, 'With Matthew Quinn, I assume?'

Fliss pressed her lips together, surprised by his attitude. 'Is that a problem?'

'Only in the sense that you apparently forgot to mention that he was the Matthew Quinn I was talking about,' he remarked coldly, and her heart dropped. Her father had gone out for a drink the evening before and Fliss had been in bed when he'd got home.

'I suppose you heard the news at the pub,' she said, turning back to the sink to hide the hot colour that had stained her cheeks.

'From at least half a dozen different sources actually,' he replied, and she knew he was hurt that she hadn't confided in him. 'D'you want to tell me how long you've known you were going to work for him?'

'Just since yesterday,' she protested, turning to rest her jean-

50

clad hip against the drainer. 'But I couldn't tell you who he was, Dad. He's come down here to try and escape the media.'

'He told you that, did he?'

'Not in so many words, no. But he said he needed some space. More space than he had in London, anyway.'

'Space!' Her father was scornful. 'Why do you young people think you need so much space? How much space did my father have when he was fighting in the trenches? The man's spent less than two years as a prisoner of war, if you want to call it that. Some of my father's men spent twice as long as that in German prison camps and there was no red carpet laid out for them when they got home.'

'I know that.' Fliss was defensive. 'In any case, I don't know what you're getting at me for. All I did was respect the man's privacy.'

George Taylor's nostrils flared. Then, as if acknowledging that she had a point, he heaved a sigh. 'I just wish you'd trusted me, that's all,' he said, pouring himself a cup of coffee from the pot. 'I can keep a confidence as well as anyone else.'

Fliss's brows arched. 'This confidence?' she asked sceptically, relieved to see he was looking a little less severe. 'Come on, Dad, you wouldn't have been able to resist it. Knowing Matthew Quinn was living in the Old Coaching House. What a scoop that would have been!'

Her father's lips pursed. 'If he'd asked me to keep his identity a secret, I'd have done so.'

'Oh, and how was he going to ask you that?' Fliss stared at him. 'You'd have had to have gone to see him. Can you imagine how I'd have felt if you had?'

'Well, it's a moot point now,' declared her father curtly. 'Harry Gilchrist couldn't wait to spread the news. I suppose that's when you saw him, too. When you went shopping in Westerbury. Was that why you forgot the netting?'

Fliss could have denied it, but there didn't seem much point. 'I suppose so,' she said, turning back to the sink. 'Anyway, I'm starting on Monday. Just mornings, I expect. Like I used to do for Colonel Phillips.'

'Huh.' Her father didn't sound too happy. 'I don't know why you insist on demeaning yourself like this. Doing other people's housework. It's not what I hoped for you, Felicity.'

'Oh, Dad!' Fliss didn't want to get into that again. 'Until Amy's older and I can go into Westerbury to work, there aren't a lot of jobs around.'

'What about working for Lady Darcy? She needs a social secretary, and I know she'd look very kindly on your application. She was only saying the other day—'

'I'm happy as I am,' said Fliss quickly, suppressing a grimace. The idea of being a companion—dogsbody—to the wife of the local member of parliament didn't appeal at all. At least what she did gave her a small measure of autonomy. Or it had when she'd worked for Colonel Phillips.

'Oh, well, don't say I didn't warn you,' declared her father casually, buttering a slice of toast, and Fliss was compelled to turn and look at him again.

'Warn me?' she echoed, regarding him with puzzled eyes. 'Warn me about what?'

'I thought you knew who he was,' said her father blandly, and Fliss's nails dug into her palms in frustration.

'I do know who he is,' she said, wondering where this was going.

'Then you'll know there have been rumours about his mental state since he got back from Abuqara,' remarked her father, reaching for the marmalade. 'Oh, here comes Amy.' His smile irritated Fliss anew. 'Hello, sweetheart. I hope you and Harvey haven't destroyed any of your mother's precious flowers.'

Amy gave her mother a rueful look. 'Not deliberately,' she said, as the retriever went to beg beside his master's chair. 'I think Harvey knocked the heads off a couple of roses, that's all.'

Fliss shook her head, but she was too disturbed by what her father had said to offer much in the way of chastisement. 'I wish you'd be more careful,' she muttered, finishing the dishes and drying her hands on a paper towel. Then, 'Do you want to come down to the Black Horse with me? I want to check on my hours for next week.'

'Ooh, yes!' exclaimed Amy, who enjoyed being fussed over by Patrick Reardon, the landlord. 'Can I?'

'May I?' Fliss corrected automatically, as her father said.

'Is that wise? Taking the child down to the pub? Do you want her to get into bad habits?'

'Like yours, you mean,' retorted Fliss tartly, but her heart wasn't really in it. What had her father meant? That Matthew Quinn had mental problems? Or was he simply using some gossip he'd heard to spoil Fliss's enthusiasm for her new job?

Whatever, Fliss decided that now was not the time to tackle him on it. Besides, on the whole, Matthew Quinn had struck her as a perfectly normal human being. OK, maybe he had problems interacting with people, but you didn't have to have been a political prisoner to feel that.

When she was younger, she'd had a similar problem. An only child, she'd been painfully shy with boys, envying girls like Diane who found it so easy to flirt with the opposite sex. No wonder Terry Matheson had taken advantage of her. She'd been ripe for the taking.

It wasn't until she'd gone to university that she'd learned to have faith in herself again. Which was why she felt such a debt of gratitude to her parents. It was also why she hated to disappoint her father now. Perhaps he was right. Perhaps Matthew Quinn did have psychological problems. But, despite his dangerous appearance, she'd liked him. And she couldn't believe Diane would be involved with someone she couldn't trust.

Nevertheless, as she cut through the churchyard on Monday morning on her way to the Old Coaching House, Fliss couldn't deny a *frisson* of apprehension. Working for Matthew Quinn was not going to be like working for Colonel Phillips. For one thing, Colonel Phillips had spent most of his days in a wheelchair. He'd spent his mornings doing the daily crossword in his newspaper, and his afternoons dozing in the conservatory that adjoined the morning room. He'd been sweet and amenable, and always willing to adapt his needs to hers.

No one would make the mistake of describing Matthew Quinn as 'sweet.' And, although he'd seemed amenable enough when he was asking her to work for him, only time would tell.

Still, if she didn't like working for him, if he proved an impossible employer, she'd be out of there. It wasn't as if she didn't have another option. Lady Darcy beckoned, and working for her might not be as bad as she anticipated.

A gate opened from the churchyard into the grounds of the house. Colonel Phillips had used it in the days when he'd attended church, but latterly Reverend Jeffreys had called at the house himself to give the old man the sacrament.

Beyond the gate, a flagged path wound around an overgrown vegetable garden before climbing steadily towards the terrace. Tall trees, ash and poplar mostly, bordered lawns badly in need of mowing. Flowering shrubs flanked the path, but they were gradually choking the life out of the perennials that grew between them.

The place needed a gardener, thought Fliss, but since Colonel Phillips went into hospital six months ago there'd been no money to pay Ray Jackson, who used to do the work. She wondered if Matthew Quinn would employ him. He didn't seem the type to do all the work himself.

Deciding he wouldn't expect her to use the front door, Fliss knocked at the back door instead. A fleeting glance through the window revealed that her employer wasn't in the kitchen. She hoped he was up. She wanted to get started.

And finished, she admitted ruefully as another shiver of apprehension rippled down her spine.

When no one answered her knock, she tried again, using a piece of wood she found beside the step instead of bruising her knuckles. A piece of Buttons's hutch, no doubt, she mused, dropping the stick again. Which reminded her she really would have to get some netting. The rabbit was still waiting for his run.

There seemed to be no movement in the house and, sighing, Fliss glanced about her. Foolishly, she'd expected Matthew Quinn to be waiting for her, ready to tell her what he wanted her to do. Instead, the place seemed deserted. Surely he hadn't forgotten she was coming?

Biting her lip, she laid her hand on the door handle, and then nearly jumped out of her skin when it opened to her touch. Just like the haunted house in that movie she'd watched with Amy, she thought, glancing behind her once again. Matthew Quinn must be up, she told herself fiercely. The door would have been locked otherwise.

Pushing it open, she stepped into the kitchen. At least this was familiar territory, and she looked around, expecting to see breakfast dishes littering the sink. But, although at some time someone had made coffee and left the dregs in the pot, it was stone cold. Clearly, he hadn't had breakfast. So where on earth was he?

'Mr Quinn!'

Moving across the tiled floor, Fliss was acutely aware of her shoes squeaking against the terrazzo tiles. Colonel Phillips had had the kitchen updated about fifteen years ago, long before she had come to work for him, and he'd chosen the décor. She supposed it was old-fashioned by today's standards, but she liked it.

'Mr Quinn!'

She called his name again as she emerged into the short corridor that led to the entrance hall. Now that she had time to look about her properly, she could see how dusty the place had become. There was even paper peeling from the wall halfway up the staircase, probably torn when the colonel's furniture had been moved out. It was a shame, but flocked wallpaper was definitely not a fashion statement these days. The whole hall and staircase needed stripping and redecorating. It would look wonderful with a fresh coat of paint and some light, cheerful wallpaper.

The hall divided the house into two parts. On one side was the drawing room and what used to be a formal dining room before Colonel Phillips had moved his bed downstairs. The old man had found the stairs difficult in recent years and Fliss had suggested the alternative arrangement.

The room was empty now, of course, as was Colonel Phillips's library at the other side of the hall and the morning room at the back of the house. She felt a little wistful when she saw the empty shelves in the library. Evidently the colonel's nephew had sold his uncle's books as well.

She didn't want to admit it, but Fliss was getting a little worried now. Where on earth was Matthew Quinn? Unwillingly, what her father had said came back to haunt her. His comments, that the man was rumoured to be unstable, were a constant drain on her confidence.

Which was silly, she told herself severely. Matthew Quinn had to be here somewhere. Perhaps he was ill. Perhaps the reason the door was unlocked was because he'd called a doctor. It wasn't so unreasonable. He had had a pretty stressful couple of years.

She paused at the foot of the stairs and called his name again. Again there was no answer, and she placed one trainer-clad foot on the bottom step. Dared she go up? Did she want to? Did she have a choice?

Of course she did, but she ignored the alternative. Taking a deep breath, she started up the stairs, assuring herself that it was what anyone else would have done in her place. After all, when Colonel Phillips had been taken ill, it was she who had called an ambulance to take him to hospital. If she hadn't had a key to the house, he would have died alone and uncared-for.

The fact that she didn't have a key now was hardly relevant. She'd surrendered her key to the solicitor when the old man died. But the door had been unlocked, she reminded herself. All she'd done was let herself in. And she was expected. She glanced at her watch. It was already a quarter past nine.

Reaching the galleried landing, Fliss paused again. She knew from experience that there were six bedrooms and three bathrooms on this floor. None of them had been used recently, but they weren't in bad decorative order. Which one would Matthew Quinn choose?

Several of the doors stood ajar so it was a fairly easy task to peer into the rooms. Like downstairs, the empty rooms stirred wistful memories. She missed Colonel Phillips. He'd been kind to her and to Amy, and they'd been fond of him in return.

The door to the back bedroom was closed and she regarded it doubtfully for a few moments before she looked into the rest of the rooms. She guessed her employer had chosen the same room as the colonel used to occupy before his arthritis got so bad. It was probably in the best state of repair.

The door to the front bedroom stood ajar like all the rest and Fliss pushed it wide enough to peer in before moving on. The curtains weren't drawn and she'd assumed the room was empty. But then her breath caught in her throat at the sight of Matthew Quinn sprawled across the mattress, his only covering a thin sheet that had wrapped itself tightly about his hips and thighs.

To her relief, he appeared to be sound asleep. Which was just as well, as the sheet was his only covering and it left little to her imagination. She tried to concentrate on the brown width of his shoulders and the hard muscles that defined his stomach. But her eyes were irresistibly drawn to the triangle of dark hair that arrowed down to his navel before disappearing beneath the low line of the bed linen.

The bones of his hips were clearly visible, his powerful legs relaxed now in sleep. Dragging her gaze away from what lay between his legs, Fliss let her eyes travel slowly up his body, lingering curiously on the silky strands of hair that grew beneath his outstretched arms. She wondered if the hair felt as soft as it looked. She knew a quite ridiculous urge to touch it and find out.

The trouble was, she had never seen a naked man before. When Terry Matheson had seduced her, it had just been a furtive fumble in the back of his car. She hadn't enjoyed it, but she had to admit she didn't know what it was like to make love with a man, to share a bed with a man. She doubted she ever would. In her opinion the whole sex thing was vastly overrated, and she fully expected to remain single for the rest of her life.

Even so, seeing Matthew Quinn like this did make her wonder what it would be like to be loved by a man like him. What would it be like to feel his hands upon her; to be kissed and caressed in places she'd never dreamed of outside of the romantic novels she borrowed from the public library? She'd always thought it was just the imagination of the author that caused the love scenes to give her such a spine tingling spasm in her stomach. The pleasurable pain she'd felt at those times had seemed almost wicked, yet she was feeling much the same sensation now, if for different reasons.

She swallowed hard. This was crazy. She shouldn't be standing here in his bedroom doorway indulging in girlish fantasies about a man she scarcely knew. Thank God, he was asleep. She didn't know what she'd do if—

But he wasn't asleep. As her hand groped for the handle of the door to pull it closed behind her, her gaze strayed to his face again—and saw his eyes were open.

At once, her face suffused with colour. Oh, lord, how long had he been awake? How long had he been aware of her staring at him? And what excuse could she give? Surely nothing she said could explain her behaviour?

There was an awkward silence while Fliss struggled to regain her composure and he blinked sleepily at her, lifting a languid arm to rake his nails across his scalp. Then, as if taking pity on her, he said, 'What time is it?' As if he didn't know she'd been ogling him for the last five minutes.

Fliss licked dry lips before replying. 'It—it's nearly half past nine,' she said jerkily. 'I—I tried the door downstairs and it was open.' She paused. 'I—wondered if you were all right.'

His dark eyes narrowed as he took in the ramifications of her statement. 'So you decided to—what? Take the time to check the place out?'

'No!' Fliss was defensive. 'When Colonel Phillips was taken ill, I was the one who found him. It occurred to me that you might be—might be—'

For the life of her, Fliss couldn't think of a way to finish her sentence without sounding melodramatic. Matthew Quinn had levered himself up on his elbows in the interim, and was now regarding her sardonically across the sunlit room. As he moved, the sheet fell a little, and her eyes dropped automatically. She wasn't a prude, but she couldn't ignore his nakedness as he apparently could.

'I'll see you downstairs,' she muttered, but, as if recognising her embarrassment, Matthew swiftly hauled the sheet up to his waist again.

'Sorry about that,' he said, not sounding sorry at all. 'I'm not used to finding strange women in my bedroom.'

'No, well, I'm sorry, too,' said Fliss, backing onto the landing. 'As I say, I'll—um—'

'I have been up, you know,' he remarked, before she could escape. 'I haven't been sleeping all that well, and I got up around five and made some coffee.'

Fliss swallowed. 'Coffee doesn't seem to be a wise choice if you're suffering from insomnia,' she offered awkwardly, and he gave her a rueful grimace.

'I guess not.' He lifted a hand to massage the back of his neck, arching his back as he did so, and once again he had to rescue the slipping sheet. 'God, what time did you say it was? Half past nine?'

'It's actually nearer twenty to ten.' Fliss corrected him a little primly and he groaned out loud.

'Dammit, that guy, Gilchrist, said the furniture would be here about ten. I'd better get dressed.'

'Take your time,' said Fliss hastily, half-afraid he was going to get out of bed before she had time to close the door. 'I'll go and make some fresh coffee.'

'Thanks,' he said, and she hurried away before he could say anything else.

CHAPTER SIX

A COUPLE of hours later, Matt surveyed his newly furnished rooms with some satisfaction.

The twin hide sofas and satin-striped armchairs he'd chosen certainly gave the drawing room a little more panache, and the antique desk and leather chair he'd bought for the library would allow him to work at his laptop in comfort, if he needed to.

Of course, he realised now he had gone about things backside first. He should have had the place redecorated before he started buying furniture, but his needs were too immediate to allow him that luxury. He needed somewhere to sit, somewhere to relax. And, after all, it wasn't as if the paper was peeling off the walls.

Except in the hall, of course. The hall and stairs would have to be tackled immediately, he acknowledged that. The impression it presently created was one of age and dilapidation.

His new housekeeper had been terrific. He had to acknowledge that, too. After providing him with toast and coffee, she'd started on the drawing room, and by the time the delivery truck arrived, albeit an hour later than he'd anticipated, both the drawing room and the library were as clean as she could make them.

She'd opened all the windows, and the pleasant smell of furniture polish mingled with the warm breeze from the garden. The windows themselves gleamed and the musty aroma of disuse that had pervaded the house had almost totally dissipated. Even the floorboards had received a coat of liquid polish and the Chinese rugs he'd bought as a temporary measure until he could get a carpet fitted looked at home on the shining floor.

If he'd had the impression that Fliss was avoiding him he'd put it down to his imagination. She was here to work, he reminded himself, trying to forget what had happened earlier. It wasn't his fault if she'd seen more than she'd bargained for. He hadn't invited her into his bedroom, for God's sake.

All the same, he couldn't deny that he'd actually enjoyed her confusion. And, for a few moments, before she'd become aware of him watching her, he'd felt a disturbing hunger in his loins. She looked so unlike any housekeeper he'd seen in her skimpy T-shirt and tight-fitting jeans, and the rush of heat that had surged into his groin had been as surprising as it had been fleeting.

It hadn't lasted. And, despite everything, he told himself he wouldn't have wanted it to. He'd do himself no favours getting involved with his housekeeper, however neutral his involvement was bound to be. She didn't know about that and he'd be a fool to indulge in sexual foreplay that could backfire on him in the most humiliating way.

Even so, that didn't stop him thinking about her. After she'd gone upstairs to tackle the bedrooms and he started unpacking the boxes of books he'd brought with him from London onto the newly polished shelves in the library, he had to admit that she intrigued him. He couldn't honestly understand why she was happy doing what she did. She was an intelligent woman, for God's sake. Didn't she want to do anything else with her life?

He supposed having Amy made her situation different from Diane's, for example. If what Diane had said was true, Fliss had given up a promising education to have her baby. But why hadn't she married the baby's father? Why was she still living at home when she must have had other opportunities to get married?

His brain baulked at the avalanche of questions. It wasn't his problem, and he had the feeling Fliss wouldn't appreciate his curiosity. Despite her occasional outbursts, he sensed she was a private person. And he couldn't forget the way she'd acted that morning when she'd found him in bed.

He was back to square one, to the very subject he didn't want to think about. Weariness enveloped him, a combination of the physical work he was doing and the mental depression he had to constantly fight against. Despite his confinement, he wasn't used to manual labour. Weeks, months spent in the confines of a small cell caused muscles to stiffen up and grow painful with lack of use. He'd tried to keep himself fit, doing push-ups and other exercises, but he'd been fighting a losing battle. Living on a starvation diet turned every effort into a major task.

Now his muscles were aching from the continual bending and lifting, and he felt an almost overwhelming desire to go back to bed. The blessed relief of oblivion beckoned, and he had to force himself to continue with his task.

A tap at the library door was not welcome. He would have preferred time to pull himself together, time to wipe his features clean of the pathetic self-pity he was feeling at this moment. But he hardly had time to straighten his shoulders before Fliss put her head round the door.

'I've made a start on the bedrooms—' she was beginning, when she caught sight of his haggard face. Her expression changed and she pushed the door wider. 'I'm sorry. I'm interrupting.' She paused, and then went on curiously, 'Are you all right, Mr Quinn?'

'It's Matt,' he said flatly, propping his hip against the rim of his desk. 'And, yeah, I'm fine. Just a little tired, is all.'

She clearly wasn't satisfied with his response. 'Are you sure?' she asked, linking her fingers together at her waist. 'You're not—well, you're not overdoing it, are you?'

Matt's lips twisted. 'Shelving books? I don't think so.'

'But you have been ill,' she pointed out reasonably, making him wonder exactly what she'd heard about him. 'I can do this tomorrow.'

'Tomorrow?'

'It's ten past one,' she offered, with a swift glance at the workmanlike watch on her wrist. 'I usually only work mornings.'

He guessed she didn't know she had a smudge of dust on her cheek or that her T-shirt had come loose from the waistband of her jeans, leaving a wedge of creamy skin to tantalise him. Didn't she realise that in his present incarnation, he was far more dangerous to both her and himself? But no. Why would she? As far as she was concerned, he and Diane...

Dragging his thoughts away from that particular minefield, he made a concerted effort to concentrate on what she was saying. 'Is that what we agreed?' he asked neutrally, folding his arms across his chest, as if by doing so he could somehow ease his aching back and subdue the emotions that were roiling inside him. 'How many mornings?'

'Well, we did agree to two days a week,' she conceded. 'We could call that five mornings, if you like. Until we see how it goes.'

'We could.' Matt considered. 'Is there some reason why you don't want to work all day?'

'I pick Amy up from school at three o'clock,' she said simply. 'And I make lunch for my father at one.'

'So you're late.'

'It's not set in stone,' she assured him quickly. 'He won't mind waiting.'

Matt arched a brow. 'He's retired, I take it?'

'More or less.' She looked a little uneasy now.

'More or less?' It was really nothing to do with him but he couldn't prevent the question. 'You mean he works part-time?'

'Sort of.'

Matt didn't say anything but she obviously realised he expected her to go on. With a little shrug, she added, 'He used to own the village pharmacy. He retired three years ago.'

Matt's brows drew together. 'I didn't realise a village of this size would have a pharmacy.'

'It doesn't now.' She hesitated. 'People go to the supermarket in Westerbury. It's cheaper.'

'So your father works in Westerbury?'

'No.' He could actually feel her frustration now, sense her unwillingness to continue. But, with a sudden gesture of resignation, she spread her hands. 'If you must know, he writes a weekly column for the local newspaper.'

Matt snapped to his feet then, gasping as his back protested the sudden move. 'Say what?' he croaked, against the pain that shot down into his thighs.

'He writes—'

'I heard you.' Matt turned and braced himself with the heels of both hands on the desk. 'Hell, no wonder you didn't want to tell me.'

'I didn't tell him about you!' Fliss exclaimed defensively. 'I could have done, but I didn't.'

'Why not?'

He heard her shift a little uncomfortably then. 'I—I didn't think you'd want me to.'

'Damn right!'

Matt attempted to move away from the desk, but for some reason his spine appeared to have locked and he couldn't deny the sudden oath that escaped his lips.

Oh, great, he thought bitterly. As well as being an emotional cripple, he was now a physical one as well. God, how had he got into this state?

'Are you all right?'

Despite her obvious unwillingness to be honest with him, Fliss came round the desk so that she could look at him. She seemed genuinely concerned about him, but Matt wasn't in the mood for her sympathy—for anybody's sympathy, actually— and the look he cast her way should have shrivelled a hardier soul than hers.

'And if I'm not? What are you going to do about it?' he snarled, wishing she would just go. He had to deal with this alone—and with the fact that anything he'd said to her up to this point could find its way into the local rag. Christ, what were the odds against him choosing the daughter of the local hack to be his housekeeper?

'I could help,' she said quietly, and with an effort he swung himself round again to rest against the desk.

'Oh, right. You're a masseuse, too, I take it? Is there no end to your ingenuity, Ms Taylor?'

She held up her head. 'I do have some experience,' she said

stiffly. 'I was training to be a physiotherapist when my mother died and I had to give up my work to look after my father and Amy.'

Matt was stunned. 'A physiotherapist?' he echoed half disbelievingly. 'But Diane said—'

He broke off, but she evidently knew what he had been about to say. 'What?' she asked drily. 'That I was a school drop-out? I was. Until I'd had Amy, that is.'

He shook his head. 'I'm impressed.'

'Don't patronise me.' Her lips tightened. 'Now, do you want me to help you or not?'

Matt shifted against the desk. 'I'm just stiff, that's all.'

'I'd say you've overdone the lifting and bending.' She contradicted him. She hesitated. 'Can you stretch out on the desk?'

Matt gave her an open-mouthed look. 'What?'

'I mean it. I'll just wash my hands.'

She headed for the door and was gone before he could stop her, and Matt made another attempt to straighten up. But the pain made him wince in agony and he wondered if he'd done something stupid like slipping a disc or trapping a nerve.

Yeah, that would figure, he thought grimly, regarding the prospect of prostrating himself on the desk with mild incredulity. But, on the other hand, he had to get mobile again.

She was back before he knew it. She came into the room smelling faintly of lemon and he guessed she'd washed her hands in the kitchen.

'Will you be warm enough if you take off your shirt?' she asked briskly, and he wondered if she had any idea what she was letting herself in for. 'But what the hell?' he muttered under his breath. She was bound to see his back sooner or later. With an effort, he managed to haul the shirt over his head, wincing only when her soft hands brushed the back of his neck.

She was trying to help him, he realised. Her nails scraped across his nape and for a moment any pain he felt melted in the raw heat of his reaction. It was as if an electrical charge had invaded his system and, for a moment, he couldn't get his breath.

Then, with a jerky movement, he swung away from her, mumbling something about not needing her assistance to take off his shirt. If she was hurt, if her cheeks turned a little pink, that wasn't his problem. He had enough to do handling the minor explosions that were arcing down into his gut.

He couldn't help but hear the way she sucked in her breath when he turned his back on her. It even made levering himself across the desk that much easier to do. He sensed she was dying to say something, but she held her tongue, and somehow he laid his shirt over the wood and spread-eagled himself upon it. He stifled a groan as he did so. Dammit, he was weaker than he'd thought.

'Right,' she said when he was lying on top of the desk, his muscles trembling from the exertion. 'If I hurt you, let me know. Just try and relax, hmm?'

Yeah, right.

Matt gritted his teeth. That was easier said than done. He reminded himself that during his first few weeks with the guerrillas, he'd been forced to march barefoot over what had felt like the roughest terrain possible, until every nerve in his body had felt as if it was on fire. His limbs had screamed for relief, but none had been forthcoming. He'd learned not to complain. That had only brought him a beating. He'd actually felt grateful when they'd thrown him into a prison cell.

So he could do this, he thought, even if the first touch of her hands on his scarred skin had him grabbing the corners of the desk, digging his palms into the sharp edges of the wood. He had to steel himself against whatever pain she inflicted; create a barrier between his conscious and subconscious self.

He soon discovered no barrier was necessary. The rhythmic kneading that began between his shoulder blades had a mesmeric effect on his brain. Her strong fingers curled into his flesh, finding and releasing the taut tendons in his neck and shoulders, splaying over his torso, moving smoothly down his spine.

He felt himself loosening, adjusting, relaxing, as that almost liquid friction probed each vertebra in turn before gliding on.

His muscles still burned, but the heat spread smoothly over him. He felt a sinuous feeling of inertia, and a mindless relief from the stiffness that had almost paralysed him minutes before.

Then, just when he was wondering what he could do to thank her, he felt her fingers slip beneath his waist and fumble for the buckle on his belt. 'Can we loosen this?' she asked, not seeming to realise he had stiffened up again. 'If you could just push your pants down around your hips, I could—'

'No!' With an effort, Matt managed to grab her hand and shove it away from him. He blew out a breath. 'What the hell do you think I am?'

'A prude?' she suggested, loosening her fingers from his and tucking them beneath her arms. She stepped back from the desk and although he sensed she was far from relaxed with him she added bravely, 'You weren't half so modest when I woke you up.'

Matt's jaw clamped, but with a supreme effort he managed to roll onto his side. 'Yeah, well…' He regarded her dourly. 'That was different.'

'Because you were calling the shots?' She didn't back off. 'I'm not about to jump your bones, Mr Quinn.'

As if she could, thought Matt grimly, pushing that thought aside to acknowledge that it was going to be bloody difficult to get down from the desk without her help. 'Look, you've done a good job,' he began, only to have her spread her hands in frustration.

'I haven't finished,' she protested. 'I haven't even touched your lumbar region, and in my opinion that's where the root of the problem lies.'

'I don't have a problem,' muttered Matt, edging uneasily across the desk and somehow swinging his legs to the floor. He winced as his body denied that statement, but he wouldn't let her see how stiff he still was. 'Thanks, anyway. I appreciate it.'

'My pleasure,' she said, though he doubted it was. She paused. 'I'll be going now. Shall I come back tomorrow?'

Matt eased himself onto his feet. 'If that's OK with you,' he said.

'OK.' She nodded. Then, with a reluctant gesture, she added, 'You'd better put your shirt on. You're sweating and you wouldn't want to catch a chill.'

'As opposed to what exactly?'

He regretted the words as soon as they were out, but Fliss had already turned away so he couldn't see her face. 'I always care about my patients,' she said smoothly, opening the door. 'I'll see you in the morning.'

The house seemed absurdly empty after she'd gone. Despite the fact that his whole purpose in coming here had been to get away from people, suddenly he missed the almost comforting awareness of her working in another part of the house.

He moved jerkily across to the windows and was in time to see her striding away down the path that led to the church. He guessed there must be a short cut through the churchyard, though, in all honesty, he didn't even know where she lived. Just that she lived with her widowed father and her daughter. That was it.

Diane would know where she lived, he acknowledged, but he had no intention of asking her. He could already imagine her reaction when he admitted that he'd employed Fliss Taylor as his housekeeper. And if she ever found out Fliss had given him a massage... She would not be pleased, but what the hell? Did he really care?

He knew he should. It wasn't Diane's fault that he'd been sent to Abuqara. It wasn't Diane's fault that he'd come back only half a man. She saw what she wanted to see. Any essential differences she either couldn't—or wouldn't—understand.

The phone rang then, startling him out of his reverie. His spirits slumped. Had his thoughts about Diane somehow communicated themselves to her? It was several days since she'd left for London and no doubt she'd expected him to ring her over the weekend.

Fortunately, there was an extension in the library so he didn't have to go far to answer the call. His reluctance as he lifted the receiver spoke volumes, but he endeavoured to inject a positive note into his voice as he said, 'Yeah, this is Quinn.'

'Matthew!' His mother's voice was so much more welcome than Diane's that Matt sagged against the bookshelves.

'Ma.'

'Are you all right?' There was concern in her voice. 'I expected you to ring me after you'd settled in.'

'I intended to.'

'Oh?' Louise Quinn's voice rose a little now. 'When, exactly?'

'Soon.' Matt sighed. 'I've been busy, Ma. Apart from the few things I brought from London, I didn't have any furniture.'

'Oh, Matthew!' There was reproof in her voice now. 'You can't possibly live like that.'

'Don't worry. I've remedied the situation.' He sighed. 'I'm not incapable, you know.'

'But after all you've been through—'

'That's in the past now.'

'Is it?' She didn't sound convinced. 'According to Diane, it's still very much in the present.'

Diane. Matt controlled the urge to say that Diane had no right to be unloading her problems onto his mother. Instead, he said evenly, 'Diane's peeved because I moved out of town.'

'And with good reason.' His mother clucked her tongue now. 'Oh, Matthew, are you sure you're going to be all right? I liked to think I was just across town if you needed me.'

'I'm fine, honestly.' Matt shifted as his back twinged again, wondering how honest he was being. 'And I'm not a million miles away. You can always come and see me. Now I have a spare bed.'

'But how are you going to look after a barn of a place like that? Diane says it has *six* bedrooms, for heaven's sake.'

Diane, again. Matt stifled his irritation and said neutrally, 'I've got a housekeeper. She's helping me get the place in order.'

'A housekeeper.' Louise sounded relieved now. 'Oh, well, that's something, I suppose. Is she going to cook for you, too?'

'I...' Matt hadn't considered the fact that he was now obliged to provide *all* his own meals. 'Possibly,' he said, wondering how Fliss would react to that suggestion. After this morning's fiasco, he'd be lucky if she didn't decide to find herself another job.

'Well, I hope so,' said his mother firmly. 'You're not fit to do everything for yourself.'

'Ma—'

'No, I mean it, Matthew. You may think you've put your past experiences behind you, but I know differently. It's all very well pretending that a person can endure years of incarceration—'

'It was one year, Ma.'

'It was nearer two.' She huffed. 'Anyway, that's not the point. No one—and I mean no one—suffers the kind of physical abuse you had to contend with and emerges unscathed.'

'I don't need this, Ma.'

'I think you do.' She was determined. 'You were starved, Matthew. Starved and beaten. God knows what other kind of mental torture they put you through—'

'For pity's sake.' Matt could feel every nerve in his body chilling with the memory. 'Do you think this is helping? Is there any useful purpose in forcing me to remember? I'm trying to forget.'

'I know, I know.' At last his mother seemed to realise how insensitive her words must sound. 'I'm sorry, darling, I'm a stupid old woman and you have every right to be angry with me. But I'm so worried about you, Matthew. We both are.'

'Both?' Matthew frowned.

'Diane and I,' said his mother impatiently. 'She was such a comfort to me while you were away. A daughter couldn't have been sweeter.'

'Yeah, well...' Matthew definitely didn't want to talk about his relationship with Diane. 'You can relax. I'm OK. Right?'

'Right.' But she still sounded uncertain. Then, injecting a note of optimism into her voice, she added, 'Anyway, at least

I'll be able to tell Diane that you've got yourself a housekeeper. I know she'll be relieved.'

Will she? Matt wanted to ask her not to mention it to Diane, but he didn't have the strength to explain why. 'I'll ring you later in the week,' he said, hoping to escape any more reproaches on Diane's behalf. 'OK?'

'You will take care, won't you, Matthew?'

'I promise,' he said, and with another brief word of farewell, he ended the call.

But, as he pushed himself away from the bookshelves and looked wearily around the library, he wondered if he was just kidding himself by thinking he could escape himself...

CHAPTER SEVEN

FOR the rest of the week, Fliss did her best to avoid her employer. She had plenty to do, and Matt himself seemed more than willing to keep out from under her feet. He didn't mention what had happened and nor did she. She hadn't forgotten the scars she'd seen on his back, but if he suspected she might tell her father he was very much mistaken.

On Wednesday morning, she arrived to find Albert Freeman, a local painter and decorator, already at work with his measuring tape and clipboard. He was only too happy to tell her that he'd been approached by 'Mr Quinn' to give him an estimate for how long it would take him to redecorate the hall, stairs and landing. Fliss knew a momentary—and totally unjustified—feeling of alienation at being cut out of the process. Matt had said nothing about his plans to her, and she consoled herself with the thought that he'd very likely find the pompous Mr Freeman rather hard to take.

However, she said nothing, getting on with her work as usual, and on Thursday morning it was Matt who came looking for her. She was cleaning out one of the store cupboards in the kitchen when his lean dark frame appeared in the doorway, and she was instantly conscious of him in every fibre of her being.

Fliss was standing on the top of the steps that had been rusting in the garden shed since old Colonel Phillips's time, and she was unhappily aware of her bare legs below the cuffs of her khaki shorts.

It was ironic really, because for most of the week she'd sweated in her jeans and T-shirt. But today it was so hot, she'd decided to go with a sleeveless vest and shorts. It wasn't as if Matt noticed what she was wearing, she'd assured herself. Most of the time, he barely seemed to notice she was there.

Except for that first morning...

But she didn't want to think of that now, not when Matt was standing staring up at her with those dark, inscrutable eyes. He was wearing loose-fitting cotton trousers and an open-necked chambray shirt folded back over muscular forearms. Both the trousers and the shirt were black and accentuated the sombre cast of his expression.

'D'you have a minute?' he asked, and she wondered with an uneasy pang if he was going to give her notice. Finding out that her father wrote a column for the weekly newspaper had definitely angered him. It was only because he'd developed those muscular pains in his back and shoulders that the subject had been dropped.

The fact that that was several days ago now didn't reassure her. He had been avoiding her, and he might have thought he had to let her work a week before finding fault with her efforts. Whatever, he was waiting for her to get down before telling her what he wanted, and, dropping the cloth she'd been using into the bucket, she turned, her foot groping blindly for the second stair.

The sudden crack as the support that had been holding the steps together snapped sounded like a gunshot in the quiet room. Almost in slow motion, it seemed, the two sides of the steps parted company, sliding away in opposite directions, leaving Fliss to flail uselessly for something to hold on to.

She was going to fall onto the steps, she knew. She couldn't avoid it. A vision of herself hitting the floor, of her limbs crumpling onto broken ribs and bare metal was all too vivid in her imagination, and there was nothing she could do about it.

It didn't happen. Somehow, Matt managed to grab her around the waist and haul her back out of harm's way. For a heart-stopping moment she was in his arms, the hard muscles of his chest and thighs pressed close to her back. Then he lost his balance and they both went down, Fliss landing heavily on top of him.

He grunted as her weight knocked most of the air out of his lungs, but for a moment Fliss couldn't move. She was so re-

lieved that she'd escaped serious injury, that she wasn't nursing
any broken bones, that it wasn't until she heard his stifled groan
that she scrambled off him.

'Oh, I'm sorry,' she cried, only just resisting the urge to run
her hands all over him. Just to reassure herself that he was still
in one piece, she told herself fiercely, ignoring the other urges
his supine form engendered in her. 'I'm such a fool. I should
have had more sense than to use those old steps!'

Matt shifted a little uneasily, as if testing his own resistance
to injury, and said weakly, 'It's not your fault. You didn't know
they were going to break at that moment. Where the hell did
you get them, anyway?'

Fliss pulled a wry face. 'From the shed.'

'Whose shed?'

'Colonel Phill—I mean, yours,' she amended lamely.
'They've been there for years.'

'I believe it.' He managed to get an elbow under his body
and levered himself up onto it. 'I guess I need some new ones.'

Fliss sat back on her heels. 'I suppose you do.' She bit her
lip. 'Are you all right? I haven't—damaged anything, have I?'

Matt's lips twitched with reluctant humour. 'Well, you're not
as light as you look,' he conceded mildly, and faint colour
entered her cheeks. He winced as he moved again. 'I may have
need of your other services, however.'

Fliss blinked. 'My other services?' she echoed, not understanding what he meant for a moment. 'What other services?'

Matt gave her a dry look. 'What are you offering?'

Fliss swallowed. 'I don't know what—'

'Physiotherapy?' suggested Matt innocently, though his eyes
were giving her a decidedly sensual appraisal. 'I'm afraid I'm
not in the market for anything else at present.'

'Oh!' Fliss's face burned. 'I wasn't—I mean I never
thought—'

'No.' His gaze had dropped to her mouth and she felt a flame
ignite deep down in the pit of her stomach. 'I know that. I was
only kidding.'

He didn't look as if he'd been kidding, she thought, knowing she should scramble out of reach before this situation got any more embarrassing. She wasn't used to this. She wasn't used to dealing with a man as sophisticated as he was, and if she wanted to save herself further humiliation she should move before he realised it.

Getting hurriedly to her feet, she said awkwardly, 'Do you need help getting up?'

'Do I look as if I do?' Matt pushed himself into a sitting position and seemed to be assessing his injuries. 'Yeah, why not?'

He held out his hand towards her and Fliss had no choice than to take it. His fingers were long and hard, his palm slightly callused—possibly the result of his incarceration. She'd read somewhere that he'd been kept in a cell barely big enough to lie down in, and she doubted he'd slept in a bed. God knew how he had kept himself sane, let alone anything else.

His hand fairly engulfed hers and she hoped he wouldn't notice how damp her skin was. Well, she had been using a wet cloth, she assured herself, hoping he'd put her sweating palm down to her exertions. But, looking into his knowing eyes, she rather doubted it.

She heaved then, stepping back as she did so, and with very little effort, it seemed, Matt came to his feet. He grunted, which might have been in protest, and clutched her other arm as he gained his balance.

'Thanks,' he said, his warm breath invading her mouth and nostrils, making what should have been a casual act of kindness into something personal and intimate. 'Are you OK?'

'Me?' The word was hardly more than a squeak and she struggled to recover her voice. 'Yes,' she said, intensely aware of his hand gripping her bare forearm. 'You—er—you cushioned my fall.'

'Oh, right.' Humour lurked at the corners of his mouth, but for some reason he didn't immediately let go of her. 'I knew it was only a matter of time before somebody used me as a doormat.'

'I didn't—' she began and then broke off abruptly, pressing

her lips together when she saw the glint in his eyes. 'I suppose you're teasing me again? It must be so satisfying to have such an easy target.'

'Sorry.' His humour disappeared and he looked down at his hand circling her arm. Was he comparing the darkness of his flesh to the paleness of hers? she wondered tensely, and then felt an unwarranted tremor in her knees when he added softly, 'I didn't mean to offend you.'

Fliss didn't know how to answer him. She was afraid her amateur efforts to defend herself had summoned an entirely too-serious response. Unless he was joking with her again. How was she supposed to know? How did women know these things? She wished she knew.

His bent head drew her unwilling gaze. He kept his hair very short, but that didn't hide how thick and springy it was, and she wondered how it would feel to run her hands over his scalp. Her fingers itched to touch him, to take advantage of this sudden, unexpected intimacy. How would he react if she behaved in a totally uncharacteristic way?

She wasn't going to find out. Not in this lifetime. She simply didn't have the courage and, besides, he would probably think she was mad. He already had a girlfriend, one far more versed in the arts of seduction than she'd ever be. Goodness, did she want to lose this job before she'd even had her first pay packet?

That didn't stop her from noticing that from this angle she could see the streaks of grey among the dark strands. Another consequence of his imprisonment, she presumed. He must have been scared at times. No matter how brave a person was, he had to have wondered if they were going to kill him. How old had they said he was in the article she'd read? Thirty-two or thirty-three? He looked older.

It was then that he lifted his head and found her looking at him. Their eyes connected, and it was like that moment in his bedroom all over again. His eyes were the same, heavy-lidded and intent, but also sensual. Her pulse quickened automatically, and she realised she should have moved away before he became aware of her interest.

She tried to do so now, but for some reason he held on, his fingers tightening about her arm. 'You're not afraid of me, are you?' he asked, as if the reaction she was exhibiting were panic. 'I've noticed you've been avoiding me all week. What has your father been telling you about me?'

'Nothing.' In all honesty, her father had been more interested in what she could tell him. 'I haven't been discussing you with him. I do have other things in my life.'

'Of course you do.' Matt pulled a wry face. 'So, when can I expect to see this article he's writing about me?'

Fliss gasped. 'He's not writing an article about you,' she protested, hoping that was true. 'You really are paranoid, aren't you? Do you think the world revolves around you?'

Matt's mouth tightened. 'I've had that impression,' he muttered.

'Well, not from me,' said Fliss staunchly, levering his fingers from her arm and stepping back. She took a deep breath. 'Now, did you want something? If not, I've got to finish these cupboards.'

Matt stared at her for another long moment and then shook his head, as if by doing so he could clear his mind of what he'd been thinking. 'Oh, yeah,' he said, raking fingers across his scalp as she'd fantasised about doing only moments before. He sighed. 'I came to ask you if you'd prefer to be paid by the week or the month.' He paused. 'It's your call.'

Fliss felt a slightly hysterical desire to laugh. His words had certainly put things in perspective. 'Am I going to be here long enough to find out?' she asked, before she could stop herself, and Matt's mouth twisted.

'Well, I want you to stay,' he said, and once again she had to struggle with the desire to ask him why.

'That's good,' she said instead. 'I—well, I had wondered.'

'Why would you do that?'

He seemed genuinely puzzled, and to add to her confusion he reached out and tucked one errant strand of fiery hair behind her ear. His fingers brushed her skin, and Fliss felt the heat explode beneath them. He had no idea what he was doing to her, she thought, and that brought her briefly to her senses.

'I—because of what you said about my father,' she stammered a little breathily, trying desperately to remember who he was and why she was here. 'You weren't exactly pleased to discover he worked for the local paper.'

'Ah.' Matt nodded, as if that explained everything. But instead of withdrawing his hand, he allowed his knuckles to trail along the curve of her jawline. 'You shouldn't take what I say so literally.' His thumb brushed her mouth, and then returned to abrade her parted lips. 'You're very trusting, aren't you, Fliss? You make me wish I were not such a burned-out husk.'

'You're not burned out,' she responded at once, and almost involuntarily her hand came up to cover his. She told herself later that she'd intended to push his fingers away, but when his thumb probed inside her mouth, all the strength drained out of her legs.

For that moment in time, she couldn't think of anything or anyone but him. The rights and wrongs of what she was doing didn't even come into it. And as if he had been startled by her unexpected action, Matt's eyes darkened, and with a muffled sound he bent towards her and replaced his fingers with his mouth.

It was just a fleeting kiss, but its effect was electric. Her lips parted instinctively, and she felt the sensuous touch of his tongue. Need, hot and totally inappropriate, invaded her system, causing her to step half-involuntarily towards him. The blood was pounding through her veins, consuming her with her own body's needs, and even the distant clang of warning bells couldn't halt the urge she had to deepen the kiss.

With goose-pimples dancing along her skin, she had no thought for Diane or anyone else. There was liquid fire in her belly and a yielding ache between her legs and for the first time in her life she understood how irresistible sexual desire could be. She'd had a taste now and she wanted more, and she uttered a little moan of protest when he abruptly gripped her upper arms and put some space between them.

'This is not a good idea,' he said thickly, and Fliss stared up into his tormented face in sudden comprehension.

Dear heaven, what was she doing? He was engaged to Diane, for heaven's sake. Whatever she thought she'd seen in his eyes was for someone else. Not her.

Her mouth was suddenly dry and she ran a nervous tongue over her lips before saying desperately, 'I'm sorry, I'm sorry.' She spread her hands wide, wishing the floor would open up and swallow her. 'I—I don't know what came over me. You're right. That—shouldn't have happened.'

'Forget it.'

His voice was harsh, but she didn't kid herself he was saying that because he felt any responsibility for what had just occurred. It was even possible that he was feeling sorry for her, and that was worse. She couldn't bear the thought that he and Diane might laugh about this behind her back.

'Look,' she said uncomfortably, 'if you'd rather I left now, I'll quite understand. I'm sure you won't have any difficulty in finding someone else to take my place.'

'Do you want to leave?'

His question startled her. 'I—it's not what I want, is it?'

'Isn't it?'

'No.' She realised she was still standing there with her arms spread and hurriedly dropped them to her sides. 'I mean, it's going to be difficult for us to work together after—this.'

'For you, you mean?'

'For you, too.' Fliss stared helplessly at him. 'All I can say is that I've never done anything like this before.'

'I believe you.' A hint of a smile touched his lips again. 'From what I've heard, your last employer was in his nineties.'

Fliss flushed. 'That's not what I meant,' she said, her fear that he might find the situation funny resurrecting itself. 'I don't—get involved with men.'

Matt held her gaze. 'Except with the man who fathered your child,' he remarked wryly. 'I'm surprised you didn't marry him if you have such conservative views.'

Fliss's lips tightened. She wasn't sure but she thought that might be an insult and she wondered what Diane had told him. And, even though she never discussed Amy's father with anyone, she felt compelled to defend herself.

'I didn't want to marry Amy's father,' she said stiffly. 'And I certainly didn't plan on having a baby at sixteen.'

'So why take the risk?' Matt's brows ascended. 'Forgive me, but you must have known what would happen, even at sixteen.'

Fliss shook her head. 'You don't understand.'

'So enlighten me.'

'Why should I?' Fliss gave him a defiant look.

'Because I'm interested.'

'Curious, don't you mean?' He shrugged, and although she suspected she was going to regret it later, she said, 'I was naive. I'd never been the kind of girl to—well, to get involved with boys. I'd always been more interested in my school work, in getting good grades.'

'Admirable.'

'Yes.' She didn't know if he was being sarcastic or not, but she went on anyway. 'I was flattered by an older boy's attentions, and I made a mistake. End of story.'

'But it wasn't the end of the story, was it?' he said. 'You had Amy.'

'Yes, I did. And Terry and his parents left the village telling everyone who would listen that he wasn't the baby's father.'

'Nice guy!'

She pulled a wry face. 'It was all for the best really. It would never have worked.' She glanced about her at the worktops piled high with goods she'd taken from the cupboards she was cleaning. 'Anyway, I'll just tidy this stuff away and then I'll go.'

Matt folded his arms across his midriff. 'Are you still annoyed with me?'

Fliss shook her head. 'No. I'm annoyed with myself.'

'Why?'

'Because I don't want you to think I regret anything that's happened.'

'Not even us sharing a kiss?'

She flushed. 'Not even that.'

His lips twisted. 'Well, don't worry about it. As you said, it's not going to happen again.'

'No, it's not.' Brushing past him, she lifted the broken steps out of the way and shoved them next to the back door. Then, lifting the bucket she had been using into the sink, she emptied the water away. 'And as far as paying me for this week is concerned, you can have it on the house.'

He muttered something that sounded suspiciously like a swear-word, but as it wasn't spoken in English she couldn't be sure. In any case, she was appalled at her own behaviour. It was all right making those kinds of gestures when you could afford it. Unfortunately she couldn't.

Matt shifted then, coming to stand with his back to the counter beside her, his frustration evident. 'Look, can't we forget all this nonsense and start again?' he demanded.

Fliss turned her head. 'You really want me to stay?'

Matt expelled a weary sigh. 'Yeah. I really want you to stay.'

She considered. 'And you won't—tell Diane what happened?'

Once again a quirk of amusement tugged at the corner of his mouth. 'No, I won't tell Diane,' he promised. Then, with a strangely mocking expression, he turned away. 'Take my word for it, she'd never believe it.'

CHAPTER EIGHT

MATT spent the rest of the day cursing himself for letting the situation with Fliss develop as it had. It would have served him right if she'd decided she didn't want to work for him after all. And, in spite of everything, he wanted her to stay.

With hindsight, he didn't know what had possessed him to act the way he had. What crazy urge had compelled him to touch her at all when he knew damn well that nothing would— or could—come of it?

OK, he understood his initial reaction when she'd landed on top of him. Having the breath knocked out of you by a warm and nubile young woman could cause a momentary loss of memory, and that was his excuse. Unfortunately, he'd prolonged the offence by holding on to her, by allowing her to believe, however briefly, that he knew what the hell he was doing.

Just because it was the first time his body had reacted normally since he came home from Abuqara, he'd wanted to prove something to himself. In those few seconds, he'd actually imagined what it would be like to ease her down onto the kitchen table and bury himself in her moist flesh, and when reality had intruded he'd fought against it.

Though not for long. His brief arousal hadn't lasted beyond the point where his brain reasserted itself. Whatever fantasy his body had entertained, his mind soon reminded him what he was capable of and what he wasn't. And making love with Fliss, however appealing that might seem in theory, clearly wasn't possible in practice. And he was a fool if he thought otherwise.

Nevertheless, for a few delightful moments, he'd enjoyed the fantasy, and that was what he regretted most. He'd let her think he wanted *her,* instead of just the dream she represented.

All the same, the memory of how soft her skin had been was a constant irritant. No, not an irritant, he contradicted himself impatiently, a torment. It reminded him of how things had used to be, how he had used to feel. Her mouth had been soft, too, moist and generous, and the intimate brush of her tongue had made him want to do more than just taste her lips.

He wondered if that was a good sign. Surely it had to be, he told himself grimly as he carried a tumbler half-filled with mature single malt out onto the patio that evening. It was significant because he hadn't felt any such emotions while he was in London. In spite of everything Diane had done to spark his interest, he'd backed away from any intimacy, and he knew she was hurt by his determination to keep her at arm's length.

The night air felt surprisingly warm. Or was that just his imagination, too? Certainly he felt a little more optimistic than he'd done for some time. Maybe this really was what he'd needed. A complete change of scene, an escape from the associations his life in London had represented. He had to believe it; had to believe that in time he'd feel like a man again.

He went to bed at ten o'clock, but he slept only fitfully. His dreams were filled with erotic images; not of Diane, as they should have been, but of Fliss Taylor, and what might have happened the day before.

The scenario was always the same: Fliss was standing at the top of the steps, long legs pale and slender, the rounded curve of her bottom prominently displayed in the khaki shorts.

His physical reaction was immediate and unbelievably carnal. Even before the steps snapped as they had that morning, he was already anticipating what she would do if he touched her, if he slid his hand over her calf and the shapely length of her thigh to the provocative cuff of her shorts. And if he slipped his fingers beneath the cuff, would she be wearing any underwear?

The crack the steps made as they broke was clearly audible, and he lunged to save her just as he'd done in reality. But there the comparison with reality ended. Instead of stumbling backward and allowing her to wind him, somehow they fell together, legs entangling, the full swell of her breasts crushed against his chest.

And his arousal was almost painful. With her lissom body moulding itself to his, his response was all-consuming. The driving urge to possess her had him rolling on top of her, parting her legs with his thigh. His hands spread over her breasts, loving the thrust of the hard peaks against his palms. He wanted to tear the sleeveless top from her, to expose her breasts to his hungry gaze, but somehow he couldn't do it. Instead he had to content himself with sucking her nipples through the thin cloth.

A haze of desire gripped him. Looking down at her, meeting her heavy-eyed gaze, he was struck anew by his own body's needs. His sex, hot and engorged, was an actual physical ache now, and he rubbed himself against her, seeking a satisfaction he desperately needed to fulfil.

It didn't happen. Like a mirage in the desert, the images faded, and a moan of real anguish escaped him as the dream slipped away. He awoke to find himself tangled in the bed sheets, one of his pillows clutched between his legs.

But this was no wet dream. Turning on to his back, he acknowledged he'd known that even while he was unconscious. He couldn't do it. He couldn't make love to a woman; any woman. He was impotent.

Pushing himself to get up, he staggered out of the bed and into the bathroom. Then, in the shower, with the water beating hot and fiery on his chilled skin, he let the memories come. The fear, the beatings, the months of isolation; they had all taken their toll. But it was the night when General Hassan had sent for him, when the disgustingly fat Arab had made it clear what he expected of him, that destroyed him still.

The horror of that night was never going to go away, he acknowledged despairingly. Even though Hassan had never laid a hand on him, he had only to think about sex and it all came back in all its sordid detail. The man had expected Matt to be flattered by his attention, that he'd welcome any chance to improve his living conditions and gain some greater comfort for himself.

As if.

Matt felt sick at the thought. But, dammit, what had he said to give Hassan the idea that he might be agreeable to his demands? What had he done to attract the interest of a pervert like him?

He guessed a psychiatrist would tell him that he hadn't done anything, that Hassan didn't need any encouragement to use his prisoners for his own amusement. He was that kind of man, that kind of monster.

Yet Matt had never told anyone about that night. Maybe if he had, he would have been able to deal with it and move on. As it was, it remained like a cancer in his soul, something he wanted to put behind him, but which refused to be ignored.

So why didn't he tell someone? he asked himself bitterly, reaching for the towel and drying himself with a savagery that spoke of his inner frustration. He'd done nothing wrong, for God's sake. He'd escaped before Hassan could force his will on him.

Matt remembered now how he had still been tied to the chair in the general's office where the guards had shackled him when the sudden sound of gunfire outside had distracted Hassan's attention. A guard had been sent to investigate and he'd come back with the news that the small town was under attack from a unit of government forces, and the general had had no choice but to go and deal with the emergency.

For a short time, Matt had been alone, listening to the uproar outside. There'd been shouting and yelling, guns being discharged into the air, apparently in all directions judging by the howls of protest that penetrated the shutters on the windows. Briefly, he'd entertained the hope that the raid had been engineered to rescue him, but that idea was extinguished as soon as Captain Rachid appeared in the doorway.

The rebel captain came into the room, closing the door behind him, and for an awful moment Matt had thought he had been sent to kill him. He couldn't think of any other reason why the man might be there, and even though they'd talked together at length, he'd been under no illusion that Rachid was his friend.

Even when the captain pulled out a knife and began cutting through the ropes that bound him, Matt had expected the worst. As soon as his hands were free, he'd made a futile attempt to attack the man, but he was weak from hunger and his arms and legs were numb from a lack of circulation.

He supposed it was a measure of the man's decency that he hadn't defended himself as harshly as he might have done. Overpowering Matt with little effort, he'd thrust his lips close to his ear and told him that a Jeep, with a full tank of petrol, was hidden around the back of the prison. By his reckoning, Matt had had less than ten minutes to find the Jeep and use it. After that, he was on his own.

In the months that followed, Matt had often wondered why Rachid had helped him. The man had been Hassan's second-in-command, a trusted ally, who had had nothing to gain by aiding him to escape.

Except, perhaps, that he hadn't approved of what his commander had intended to do. Matt knew he would never know now. Rachid had been killed during the final battle for Abuqara City, and Hassan had been arrested some time later for crimes against the state. The only positive outcome had been the change of government, brought about by external pressure when the rebellion was quashed, but he doubted there would be any fundamental change of policy.

Nevertheless, he owed a tremendous debt of gratitude to the rebel captain. Without his intervention—and Matt had come to believe there never had been any government forces in the area—he'd never have got away.

So why was he so unwilling to talk about it? He had nothing to be ashamed of. He scowled. The truth was, he *was* ashamed. Ashamed of his own weakness; of his helplessness in the face of danger; of the stupidity he'd displayed in letting such a thing happen to him.

And, even though he knew it was crazy, he couldn't confess

his deepest fears to a total stranger and there was no oné else. If his father had still been alive, he might have been able to talk to him, but Alistair Quinn had died while his son was in captivity. Another burden Matt had had to bear since he got back.

Discussing his imprisonment with his mother had been out of the question. Louise would have been horrified at the news that her son had suffered any kind of brutality at the hands of his captors. She hadn't even wanted to see the scars on his back, that had had to be treated at a hospital and which some news hack had found out about and made such a big thing of. She'd been delighted to have him home. But she definitely didn't want to be reminded of what might have gone on while he was away.

Diane had remained the only possibility, but she had quickly diverted him from any discussion of the squalid conditions he'd had to suffer. Like his mother, she didn't want to think about the past. She wanted to talk about the future, their future. A future, Matt now acknowledged, that had never seemed more remote.

He dressed in a cotton vest and drawstring sweat pants and was drinking his first coffee of the day when Fliss knocked at the back door. He knew it was her. He could see her shadow through the windowed half-panels in the door, and, although he could have done with a little more time to regain his composure before seeing her again, he had no choice but to let her in.

She wasn't alone. To his surprise, when he opened the door, Amy was standing at her mother's side. They were both dressed in shorts and T-shirts, Amy's hair, which was longer than her mother's and straighter, caught up in a pony-tail.

'Hi, Quinn.'

Predictably, it was Amy who spoke first and Matt saw the way Fliss winced at her daughter's familiarity. But she had evidently decided to put what had happened the day before behind her and her tone was coolly polite as she said, 'Amy's got a day's holiday today. I hoped you wouldn't mind if she came and played in the garden while I'm working.'

'No.' Matt took a step back, silently inviting them inside. 'I don't mind at all.' His eyes moved to the child and he managed a grin. 'Hello again, Amy. Or are you calling yourself something else today?'

Amy giggled. 'Well…' she said thoughtfully, putting a finger against her lips, but her mother intervened.

'Amy will do,' she said firmly, stepping inside. She glanced behind her. 'Don't go out of the garden, will you, Amy? And if you want anything, come and knock at this door.'

'She can come and have a drink,' said Matt, not quite knowing why he'd made the suggestion, but clearly Fliss thought she did.

'It's not necessary,' she said, her cheeks a little pink. 'I'll be starting work straight away—'

'Well, as I've just made a pot of coffee, why don't we all have a drink first?' suggested Matt drily, and Amy gave him a huge smile.

'Oh, yes, Mummy. Can we?'

She was obviously eager and Fliss, finding herself outvoted, had little choice but to give in. All the same, Matt noticed that she ignored his offer of a seat and took her coffee standing, her hip firmly wedged against the counter behind her.

And, conversely, he found himself resenting her behaviour. A few moments ago, he hadn't wanted to open the door to her, and now he was finding her polite detachment hard to take. Dammit, he regretted what had happened just as much as she did. More, probably. And she hadn't had to contend with erotic dreams that had tormented his sleep and left him feeling strangely off-key.

'Grandad's going to make a bigger place for Buttons,' Amy offered, after Matt had handed her a glass of fizzy lemonade.

'An enclosure,' corrected Fliss and Amy nodded.

'Yes. A "closure."' She glanced about her. 'Do you have a straw?'

'Amy!'

Fliss was impatient, but Matt was grateful to the child for lightening the mood. 'Sorry,' he said, pulling a wry face. 'But I'll be sure and have some for next time.'

Amy beamed. 'Colonel Phillips used to buy straws just for me,' she said proudly. 'Did you know Colonel Phillips? He was very old.'

'Amy,' Fliss said again, but Matt was happy to continue the conversation. At least with Amy there were no undercurrents; no suspicion that Fliss had only agreed to stay to prove something to herself.

'No, I didn't know Colonel Phillips,' he said, wishing Fliss would sit down so he could do the same. He could feel an ache in his lumbar region, which he guessed was the result of the fall he'd taken the day before. 'He was gone before I bought the house.' He paused. 'Did he let you come here with your Mummy, too?'

'Oh, yes.' Amy spoke airily. 'He used to like me to come and play games with him. Board games, I mean. Draughts and ludo, that sort of thing. Oh, and he had boxes and boxes of coins and stuff. I used to like looking at them.'

'I bet.' Matt's eyes moved thoughtfully to Fliss's solemn face and then away again. What was she thinking? he wondered. That he was using the child to find out more about her? He considered. 'I'm afraid I don't have any coins, but I do have lots of books that need sorting out. How would you like to help me this morning? We could sort them out together.'

'It's a fine morning,' said Fliss at once. 'Amy will be happy enough in the garden. You don't have to entertain her, Mr Quinn.'

'I know I don't,' said Matt, and, seeing the little girl's disappointed face, he couldn't help responding to it. 'But I mean it. Amy can help me. You saw how many boxes of books there are.'

'I'm a good reader,' put in Amy at once. 'Mrs Hill says I'm the best reader in my class.'

'Brilliant,' said Matt, with a rueful grin at Fliss. 'You don't mind, do you?'

Fliss allowed a sigh to escape her. 'I—of course I don't mind, but—'

'That's settled, then,' said Matt, and, deciding there was no point in being proud, he sank gratefully into a chair at the table. 'I'll be glad of her help, and if she gets bored she can always go outside.'

'I won't get bored,' declared Amy, but Matt could see that Fliss still had her doubts.

'If you need help…' she began, but he shook his head.

'She'll be good company,' he assured her. If only because she would stop him from dwelling on other things. 'We'll be fine.'

'Well, it's very kind of you,' Fliss said awkwardly, and he glimpsed a trace of empathy at last. She finished her coffee and put down her cup. 'I'll leave you to it, then.' She bent and gave Amy a kiss. 'You be good now,' she added. 'And don't get in Mr Quinn's way.'

The morning passed remarkably quickly. Matt hadn't exaggerated when he'd said that Amy would be good company. She was. She liked to talk. She chattered on about everything, from school and her family to what she'd watched on television the night before. And he discovered she wasn't at all inhibited about the fact that she didn't know her father.

'He went away before I was born,' she said matter-of-factly, spilling books, that Matt had just sorted into categories, over his desk. 'Where do you want me to put these?'

'Oh—just leave them where they are,' said Matt resignedly, beginning to sort them all over again. 'You open that box over there. You might find something interesting in it.'

Amy went to squat beside the box he'd indicated, and Matt wondered if she'd say any more about her father. But she didn't. Instead, she used the scissors to cut the string that bound the box, and then hauled out the first of the photograph albums that were inside.

'Is this yours?' she asked, and Matt nodded.

'It's a kind of picture record of the different stories I used to report for *Thames Valley News,*' he explained. 'I thought you might find it more interesting than all these reference books.'

Amy's eyes widened. 'Did you used to work on television?' she exclaimed. 'Oh, wow! That's so cool.'

'It was just a job,' said Matt modestly, finding her innocent admiration much more appealing than the insincere flattery he'd received from various quarters since he'd got back. All the same, he didn't deserve it, and to divert her he bent and pointed to a man pictured in one of the stills. 'Did you know he used to be the President of Abuqara?'

Amy stared. 'Have you met him?'

'Oh, yeah.' Matt's jaw tightened and he wondered why he'd bothered to bring Abraham Adil to her attention. 'That was why I was in Abuqara. To report on the rebellion that was trying to get rid of his administration.'

'And did they?' Amy asked, her interest as innocent as her praise, and Matt sighed.

'Get rid of the government?' And after a quick nod of assent, 'Eventually.' He pulled a face. 'Unfortunately, the new government is likely to be just as corrupt.'

'Corrupt?' Amy frowned.

'Bad,' amended Matt, straightening again with an effort. 'There are oil reserves in Abuqara and everyone wants to control them. Not always for humanitarian reasons.'

Amy clearly didn't understand now, and he realised he shouldn't be talking of such things to her. She didn't understand. How could she? In her world—thank goodness—people didn't lie and cheat and torture to gain their own ends.

'Was it this man who put you in prison?' she asked suddenly, and Matt caught his breath.

'Who told you I'd been in prison?' he demanded, feeling unexpectedly betrayed. 'Your mother?'

Amy wouldn't look at him now. 'No one told me,' she muttered, turning another page of the album and pretending to be interested in a picture of sand-dunes. 'Is this in Abuqara, too?'

Matt sighed. 'Amy,' he said sternly. 'How did you find out?'

Amy glanced at him then, her brows arched in artless enquiry. 'How did I find out what?'

'Amy!'

She sighed. 'If you must know, I heard Grandad talking to Mummy,' she admitted in a low voice. 'He was annoyed because she hadn't told him who you were.'

Matt hesitated. 'And do you know who I am, Amy?'

She gave a careless shrug. 'Yes.'

'So who am I?'

'You're Matthew Quinn,' she responded at once. 'You told me who you were.'

'Mmm.' Matt considered her answer. 'I suppose I did. Not that it matters. The whole village probably knows I've bought this place.'

Amy's brows drew together again. 'Do you mind?' she asked, and he was unwillingly touched by her sincerity. 'Are you ashamed because they put you in prison?'

'No.' Matt wished it were that simple.

'So why did they put you in prison? What did you do wrong?'

Matt sighed. 'In Abuqara, you don't have to do anything wrong to be put in prison.' He grimaced. 'If you're in the wrong place at the wrong time, you don't have a choice.'

Amy put the photograph album aside. 'And you were in the wrong place at the wrong time?'

'Yeah.'

'So why don't you want people to know where you are now?' she asked practically, and he couldn't prevent a wry smile.

'Do you know what the media is?'

Amy shook her head. 'No.'

'Well, it's newspapers and magazines and television reporters—'

'Like you?'

'Like I used to be,' he admitted honestly. 'Since I got back, they've all wanted a piece of me.'

'A piece of you?' Amy was perplexed. 'You mean, they want to cut you up?'

In a manner of speaking, thought Matt drily, but he didn't say it. 'I mean, they all want a story—my story,' he said instead. 'I guess getting kidnapped by guerrillas is news. They want to know how I survived it.'

'Gorillas?' said Amy curiously. 'Why would gorillas want to kidnap you? Did they hurt you?'

Matt couldn't help himself. He laughed, and, seeing his amusement, Amy laughed, too. For a few moments, they were both convulsed with mirth, and it was only when the door opened and Fliss appeared that Matt realised she must have heard them and wondered what on earth was going on.

'Is everything all right?' she asked, and Matt made an effort to control himself. But it was the first time he'd laughed so unrestrainedly since he got back from Abuqara, and it felt good. Really good.

'Everything's fine,' he said now, as Amy scrubbed the heels of her hands over her wet eyes. 'Amy said something funny, that's all.'

'Did you know Quinn was kidnapped by gorillas?' asked the little girl, trying to stifle her giggles, and Matt saw the look of comprehension that crossed her mother's face.

'Guerrillas, Amy,' she said, and then, as if realising she was being too pedantic, she shook her head.

'Well, I can see you've been having a good time,' she remarked wryly. 'Are you ready to go home now?'

Amy's face dropped, and even Matt felt a reluctance to let her go. 'Is it that time already?' he asked, gazing at his watch in disbelief. 'I had no idea.'

'Do we have to go, Mum?' protested Amy. She hurriedly picked up the album again and opened it at the page showing the picture of Abraham Adil. 'Look, that's the President of Abuqara. Quinn says he knows him.'

'Really?' Fliss barely glanced at the picture before looking at Matt again with concerned eyes. 'You haven't been telling

Amy about—well, about your experiences, have you?' she asked tightly, and he gave her a narrow-eyed look.

'Oh, yeah,' he said. Then, seeing her dismay, he relented. 'What do you think I am? Crazy?'

'Of course not.' Her response was automatic, but he couldn't make up his mind whether he believed her or not. And, dammit, he hadn't exactly given her a good impression of himself so far.

'Look, we were just talking, that's all,' he muttered gruffly. 'If anything, I was giving her a history lesson. About the problems in North Africa.' He paused and then continued wearily, 'She already knew I'd been in prison. Perhaps you ought to ask her how she knew about that.'

CHAPTER NINE

FLISS had to work at the pub that evening.

She didn't feel like it, particularly after the way she'd left the Old Coaching House that afternoon. She felt on edge and uneasy, ready to snap at the first wrong word. But, although she would have liked to blame Matt for her bad mood, she knew it wasn't his fault that she felt so depressed.

Yet it seemed that every time she and Matt seemed to be making some progress, something happened to upset the balance. This time, it was what Amy had overheard—and apparently related to him—and she hadn't known what to say when he'd accused her of gossiping about him at home.

Of course, his response had been triggered by her reaction to Amy's excitement over the photographs. She'd immediately jumped to the wrong conclusion and there was no excuse for that. But, dammit, her fears had been fuelled by what her father had told her. If he hadn't filled her head with what he'd heard about Matt's supposed instability, she'd never have suspected him of telling Amy horror stories in the first place.

Not that those things weren't constantly on her mind, too, she conceded unhappily, heading back to the restaurant to take another order. Although she'd attempted to convince herself that the scars she'd seen on his back looked worse than they actually were, the images they'd evoked simply wouldn't go away. What had he done, for God's sake, to deserve such punishment? What kind of monster had done that to him? Did anyone ever recover from that kind of experience?

'Hello, Fliss.'

Someone spoke, a man, and Fliss, who had been concentrating on adding the table's number to her order pad, looked up in surprise.

Harry Gilchrist was one of the four young people who had recently been shown to a table in the window. He and another man Fliss knew by sight were sitting opposite two young women she didn't recognise. Pasting on a friendly smile, she returned his greeting and then said, 'Are you ready to order?'

'What are your specials?' asked the other man, nodding towards the extra dishes that were posted on a board beside the bar. He raised his eyebrows at his companion. 'I fancy a steak.'

'Do you?' she said archly. 'I fancy something else entirely.'

Fliss ignored this and recited the evening's special dishes, but she could see that Harry wasn't comfortable with his friends' behaviour. 'Are you OK, Fliss?' he asked, showing her the kind of attention he should have been showing his girlfriend. 'I heard you'd gone to work for our local celebrity. What's he like?'

Fliss's lips tightened. 'You should know, Harry. I saw you talking to him yourself the other afternoon.'

Harry looked a little put out now and Fliss knew she shouldn't have taken her bad mood out on him. 'I only meant what's he like to work for,' he muttered. 'He's bit of a weirdo, isn't he?'

'Who, Matthew Quinn?' asked his male companion with interest. 'I didn't know you knew him, Gil.'

'I don't,' said Harry shortly, giving Fliss a resentful look. 'He came into the store, that's all.' He paused, before returning to his earlier comment. 'That's what I've heard, anyway.'

'Well, you heard wrong,' said Fliss, her nails digging into her pad. 'Now, have you decided what you want to eat or shall I come back?'

She was flushed when she got back to the kitchen and Eileen Reardon regarded her curiously. 'Is something wrong, love?' she asked, her gentle Irish brogue soft with concern. 'I saw Harry Gilchrist come in. What's he been saying to you?'

'Oh—nothing.' Fliss couldn't let Eileen think Harry was to blame. In all honesty, he had only been trying to be friendly, as always. 'I—it's very warm in there, that's all.'

'Are you sure?'

Eileen was looking at her with such compassion in her eyes that Fliss was tempted to confide in her. This was when she missed her mother most. Her father did his best, but he was a man. He didn't always understand how she was feeling.

But she didn't have the right to discuss Matt's affairs with anyone, and, forcing a rueful smile, she said, 'It's been a long day. Thank goodness it's the weekend.'

Eileen hesitated. 'Is the job at the big house getting too much for you?'

'Oh—no.' Once again, Fliss's colour deepened. 'Um—I'd better give these orders in,' she added, easing past her employer's wife with some relief. 'Or your customers will be complaining.'

Eileen let her go, but Fliss knew she wasn't entirely satisfied with her answer. She hoped the older woman thought it was just because she was tired. She would hate any more gossip to find its way to Matt's ears.

Fliss had hoped to stay in bed a little later the next morning, but at seven o'clock Amy came bounding into the room. She'd taken to copying her mother's example and sleeping in cotton boxers and a T-shirt, and now she bounced onto the bed and crossed her bare legs.

'It's another lovely morning, Mum,' she announced brightly, as her mother struggled to get her bearings. 'Do you think we could go to the beach?'

'The beach?' Fliss shook her head in some bewilderment. She'd slept only fitfully again and she was having trouble in assimilating the fact that it was Saturday and she didn't have to go to work. 'Oh, I don't know...'

'Come on, Mum,' Amy was pleading. 'You know we always have a good time at the beach. And we haven't been for ages and ages.'

'At least a month,' agreed her mother drily. 'Amy, I've got housework to do. And shopping. You can come into Westerbury with me, if you like.'

'I don't want to go shopping,' said Amy moodily. 'We always go shopping. I wanted us to have some fun together.

Kelly Mason says that her mum and dad always take her out at weekends.'

Fliss expelled a weary breath and eased up against her pillows. She could have pointed out that Kelly Mason's mother had all week to do her household chores. She didn't have a job outside of looking after her husband and family, but Amy didn't want to hear that.

Besides, Fliss had to admit she was right. She did usually spend Saturdays shopping or working in the garden, and it was only natural that Amy resented her preoccupation with such matters. But going to the beach...

'How about having lunch at McDonalds?' she compromised, knowing Amy loved eating out, but the little girl only picked disconsolately at a thread hanging off the bed sheet.

'I'm not hungry,' she muttered, pursing her lips, and Fliss sighed.

'Amy—'

'It doesn't matter,' she said indifferently, sliding off the bed. 'I'm going to give Buttons his breakfast.'

Which was something else she had to do, Fliss reminded herself, unable to suppress a yawn. Unless she got some netting, the rabbit's enclosure would never be made. Her father had made his order and he wouldn't do anything else until she supplied the materials.

With a feeling of tiredness that had little to do with her restless night, Fliss swung her legs out of bed and got up. When she opened her bedroom door she found that her father had beaten her into the bathroom. She could hear the shower running, and, realising he was going to be some time yet, she went downstairs to use the toilet there.

There was no sign of Amy, but she wasn't worried. Although the child was unlikely to have got dressed before she went out, it was a warm, sunny morning and she'd come to no harm going outside in just her sleeping shorts and T-shirt. Besides, Harvey was obviously with her, and he'd bark if anyone was about.

After attending to her immediate needs, Fliss washed her

hands and then spooned coffee grains into the filter. With the reassuring sound of the coffee straining into the pot, she linked her hands together and stretched her arms above her head.

It was so good to feel her spine expanding, to feel all the kinks disappearing beneath a sudden wave of well-being. At least she was fit and healthy, she reminded herself firmly, her spirits lifting. She should be grateful for that.

She frowned as she looped one arm over her shoulder to meet the arm she'd twisted behind her back. Perhaps she and Amy could go to the beach, after all. She was up early enough, goodness knew. If she hurried and got her chores done straight after breakfast, she could leave the shopping until they got back.

She was reversing the exercise when the back door opened behind her. Guessing it was Amy, she didn't immediately turn to look at her. She was too busy anticipating how delighted her daughter was going to be when she broke the news, and only when the cooler air from outside drifted about her bare midriff did she say, 'Can you close the door, Ames? Please.'

She was arching her back in a final stretch when a disturbingly familiar male voice said, 'Amy's coming. She's just checking on the rabbit, I think.'

Immediately, Fliss abandoned her exercises, and swung round to face him. 'What are you doing here?' she demanded, the shock of being discovered in her night wear briefly obscuring the fact of how unusual it was for him to leave the house. 'Where's Amy?'

Matt tucked his fingers beneath his arms, an expression of mild amusement giving his dark features a disturbingly sexual appeal. Like her, he was wearing shorts, though she guessed he hadn't slept in his. And a black vest, that revealed surprisingly muscled biceps for a man who supposedly led a sedentary life. Just looking at him like this made her toes curl, and the ache down in her belly caused a moist heat to make itself felt between her legs.

'As I said before, she's coming,' Matt declared, his eyes

surveying her just as thoroughly as she was surveying him. 'I think she wanted me to speak to you first.'

Fliss's heart sank. 'What's she done now?' she asked wearily, deciding she couldn't worry about her appearance right now. What she was wearing was decent enough, even if her nipples were etched unmistakably against the thin cloth of her T-shirt. 'Don't tell me she's been annoying you again.'

'As far as I'm aware, Amy has never annoyed me,' he retorted, emphasising the last two words. 'I like her. She's a good kid.'

Fliss breathed through her nose, trying to subdue the erratic beat of her heart. 'I know that,' she said. 'Unfortunately, that doesn't stop her from getting into mischief.' She paused, and then, as the reality of his presence registered, 'I'm sorry. Were you looking for me?'

Matt sighed. 'In a manner of speaking, I guess.'

Fliss frowned. 'You haven't come here to speak to my father, have you?'

'Unlikely.' Matt's lips twisted. 'My information was that he isn't up yet.'

'From Amy?' Fliss blew out an exasperated breath. 'Well, sorry to disappoint you, but he is up. He's in the bathroom, but I have every reason to believe he'll be down here any minute now.'

'Magic.' Matt pulled a wry face. 'OK, here's what I came to say—Amy tells me you don't have time to take her to the beach—'

'Amy told you that?'

'Yeah.' Matt shifted his weight from one foot to the other. 'All right, I'll admit it. She did come over to the house. The dog—what's its name? Harvey?—had got into the garden and she was looking for it.'

Fliss snorted. 'Yeah, right.' She gave him a pitying look. 'Believe me, if Harvey was in your garden, Amy must have put him there. There's no way he could get out of this garden without someone opening the gate.'

'Perhaps she was taking him for a walk?' suggested Matt mildly, but Fliss only made another impatient gesture.

'In her nightclothes?' she demanded scornfully, and Matt gave a lazy shrug.

'Why not? You apparently do aerobics in yours.'

Fliss felt the colour flood into her throat. 'In my own kitchen,' she retorted indignantly, and his lean mouth tilted in an incredibly sexy grin.

'OK,' he conceded. 'That wasn't fair. I'm sorry. But it's true, isn't it? You did tell Amy you couldn't take her to the beach.'

'I might have done.'

Matt waited a beat. Then, he said, 'I wondered if you'd allow me to take her out.'

'You?'

Fliss was taken aback and it showed, and Matt's mouth compressed. 'Yeah,' he said flatly. 'I knew it was a crazy idea, but I had to run it by you.' He half turned. 'Forget it. I'll see you Monday morning at the usual time—'

'Wait!' Fliss didn't know what possessed her, but she couldn't let him go like this. 'I—let me think about it, at least.'

Matt paused, and eyes dark as sin impaled her with a sceptical look. 'What's to think about?' he asked. 'You hardly know me. I know that. You don't know if you can trust me. Like I said, it was a crazy idea. Why don't we both forget I ever mentioned it?'

Fliss shook her head. 'I can't do that.'

'Why not?'

'Well—for a start, because I do think I can trust you.'

'Thanks.' His tone was dry.

'I mean it.' Fliss sighed. 'But Amy had no right to involve you—'

'If you say so.'

'—and I'm sure you have better things to do than take a nine-year-old to the beach.'

'Ah.' He was sardonic. 'This is your way of letting me down gently, right?'

'Wrong.'

'But you're going to say no, anyway,' he persisted harshly. 'Why don't you just come out and say so?'

'If you must know, I'd already decided to take her myself,' said Fliss defensively, and she saw the way his mouth turned down at this news.

'Yeah, right.'

'I mean it.' She gave a helpless shake of her head. 'Why would I lie?'

'You tell me.'

'I'm not lying,' she protested. 'If you don't believe me, why don't you come with us?'

It was one of those moments when the air in the room practically shimmered with tension. Matt was obviously taken aback by her words and Fliss was wondering how much deeper a hole she was going to dig herself. Dear God, she didn't want to spend a whole day with him any more than he wanted to spend the day with her. Dammit, why hadn't she kept her big mouth shut?

'What's going on here?'

Her father's appearance in the doorway seemed like the last straw. She had hoped Matt would have said his piece and disappeared before her father came down, but now George Taylor was staring at their visitor with wary eyes. He'd recognised him, of course. How could he not? And he was characteristically suspicious as to why Matt should be standing in his kitchen.

In fact it was Matt who took the initiative. 'Mr Taylor, I presume,' he remarked easily, putting out his hand to shake the other man's as if he'd never expressed any reluctance to speak to a member of the Press. 'Matt Quinn. I'm the new owner of the Old Coaching House.'

'I know who you are Mr Quinn,' said Fliss's father stiffly, obviously as taken aback by Matt's cordiality as Fliss was herself. Then his gaze turned to his daughter, and his lips tightened. 'I suggest you go and put some clothes on, Felicity. I'll entertain our guest.'

Fliss rolled her eyes. 'Dad—'

'It's OK,' said Matt, before she could say anything more. 'I've got to go and finish my breakfast and lock up the house.' He met Fliss's gaze with apparent unconcern. 'I'll leave your daughter to explain that I'm taking her and your granddaughter out for the day.'

Fliss didn't know which of them was the most shocked, her or her father. But rather than wait to see how she was going to handle it, Matt arched a challenging brow in her direction and headed for the door.

'I'll be back in an hour,' he promised blandly. 'Nice to meet you, Mr Taylor.'

And with that, he was gone, and Fliss was left to face her father's undoubted irritation. The door had scarcely closed behind Matt before he snapped, 'Do you want to tell me what's going on between you and that man? Why would he think he had the right to come here at—' he consulted his wrist-watch before continuing—'at seven-thirty in the morning? Has he been here all night?'

Fliss's jaw dropped. 'Don't be ridiculous!'

'What's ridiculous about it? I didn't hear a car, and you're hardly dressed to receive visitors.' His lips pursed with annoyance as he viewed her attire. 'And couldn't you buy yourself some nightgowns? What must he think, finding you wearing men's underpants to sleep in?'

'They're boxers,' Fliss corrected him shortly. 'And they're very comfortable, actually.'

'No doubt.' Her father sniffed. 'Well? What's all this about?'

Fliss expelled an exasperated breath, but before she could answer the door opened again and Amy and Harvey bounded in. 'Is it true?' the little girl demanded as Harvey raced wildly about the room. 'Are we really going out with Quinn? He said we were. He said you'd said we could all go to the beach.'

'Amy—'

'I think your mother's taken leave of her senses,' retorted her grandfather dauntingly. 'I never approved of her going to work for that man, but getting you involved as well—'

'I didn't get Amy involved,' protested Fliss quickly, not prepared to be blamed for something that really wasn't her fault. 'It was Amy who let Harvey into Matt's garden.'

'So it's "Matt's" garden, is it?' Her father was scornful. Then he turned to his granddaughter. 'Is this true, Amy? Did you let Harvey out?'

Amy hunched her shoulders. 'I might have done.'

'Either you did or you didn't.' Her grandfather regarded her sternly. 'You know that was a very naughty thing to do, don't you? Harvey could have run away, or got knocked down. Anything.'

'No, he couldn't,' muttered Amy sulkily. 'He was safe enough in the garden at the big house.'

Her grandfather gasped. 'So, you admit you deliberately released the dog in Mr Quinn's garden?'

Amy looked mutinous. 'He didn't mind.'

'How do you know that?' Fliss's father was angry now. 'You hardly know the man.'

'I do, too.' Amy was defiant. 'I spent all yesterday morning talking to him.' She took a breath and then added staunchly, 'He likes me.'

'Does he?' George Taylor turned back to his daughter now. 'Why wasn't I told about this?'

Fliss sighed. 'About what?'

'About Amy spending the morning with that man,' stated her father grimly. 'I thought you told me she was going to play outside, as she used to do when you worked for the colonel—'

'I didn't always play outside,' Amy interrupted him quickly, and although Fliss knew the child was only trying to defend herself, she wasn't doing herself any favours by reminding her grandfather of that. He had always been jealous of the time Amy spent with Colonel Phillips, and of the affection she had had for the old man. 'We often used to play games—'

'Be quiet, Amy.' Her grandfather had heard enough. 'Well, Fliss? I'm waiting for an answer.'

'You're not talking to Amy now, Dad,' retorted Fliss, deciding her own grievance with her daughter would have to wait.

'Amy was helping Mr Quinn unpack some books, that was all. He was glad of her company.'

'And you left her with this man? With a man you hardly know?' Her father shook his head. 'I thought you'd have had more sense!'

Fliss stared at him. 'What's that supposed to mean?'

'Oh—' He swung away to lift his coffee mug from the hook and poured himself a cup before saying anything else. Then, aware that she was still watching him, he muttered, 'I should have thought it was obvious.'

Fliss felt cold. 'I hope you don't mean what I think you mean,' she began, and Amy looked confused.

'What does Grandad mean?' she asked innocently, and Fliss realised she couldn't say anything more in front of her daughter.

'Your grandfather's just feeling liverish,' she said instead, deciding getting dressed would have to wait until after breakfast. 'Now, I suggest you go and put your clothes on. I'll get my shower after you've finished.'

Amy moved reluctantly towards the door and Fliss was hardly surprised when she paused in the doorway. 'We are going out, aren't we, Mummy?' she asked anxiously. 'You're not going to say no because Grandad's cross?'

Fliss blew out a breath. 'Just get dressed, Amy,' she advised the little girl flatly, but Amy was persistent.

'Are we?' she pleaded. 'Please say we are.'

'I'll think about it,' said Fliss, giving her father a reflective look. 'Now, scoot.'

'Can I wear my new skirt?'

'Don't push your luck,' Fliss declared drily, and the child had to be content with that.

But after Amy had disappeared upstairs, Fliss turned from taking milk from the refrigerator and said, 'Why are you being so horrible about this? What have I done to make you think I can't look after myself and my daughter?'

Her father pulled out a chair at the table and then shook his head. 'You can ask me that?'

Fliss caught her breath. 'I was sixteen, Dad.' She paused. 'I thought we'd got over that.'

'We have,' he muttered, setting his mug on the table and then dropping wearily into his chair. 'But dammit, Fliss, I've told you what I've heard about that man.'

'And what have you heard exactly?'

'Just what I said—that he's had some mental problems since he got back from Abuqara.'

'What kind of mental problems?'

'I don't know.' Her father took a mouthful of his coffee. 'God knows what state he was in when he got back.'

Fliss sighed. 'Isn't this just gossip?'

'Well, you said yourself he'd left London because he felt he needed space.'

'So?'

'So—why would he do that? I mean, as I hear it, the company he worked for were more than willing to give him his old job back.'

'Perhaps he felt like a change.'

'Yes.' Her father reached for the morning newspaper Fliss had picked up from the hall when she came down. 'Well, in my opinion, no one in their right mind would have turned down the opportunity to pick up where they had left off. Most wouldn't get the chance.'

Fliss lifted a loaf from the bread bin. 'Perhaps that was because he was good at his job,' she said practically, but her father wasn't having that.

'And perhaps it's because he knows he can't hack it anymore,' he retorted shortly. 'Grow up, Fliss. The man's a kook, and if you can't see it, you don't deserve to have responsibility for an impressionable child like Amy.'

CHAPTER TEN

MATT wasn't sure whether he'd expected Fliss to back out of the arrangement or what. It had been obvious that her father hadn't been pleased to find them together and no doubt he exerted quite a lot of influence on her life. And, although Fliss had offered the invitation, he had the feeling she'd expected him to refuse.

What he definitely hadn't expected, however, was that she and Amy would turn up on his doorstep less than an hour later carrying backpacks and a cooler. Fliss's face was flushed and even Amy looked a little less exuberant than usual, and he wondered what had been said after he'd left.

'Hi, Quinn.' As usual, Amy was the first to speak. 'Are you ready to go?'

Matt frowned. 'I can be,' he said, his eyes on Fliss's face. Then, 'You could have used the front door, you know.'

'We walked,' said Fliss, and he could tell by her tone that she was embarrassed to admit it. 'Um—my father's decided he needs the car today.'

'No problem. We can use mine.' Matt stepped back. 'Come on in. The coffee's still hot. Help yourself to a cup while I put some shoes on.'

'Do you have any more of that lemonade I had yesterday?' asked Amy at once, dumping her backpack just inside the door and looking expectantly round the kitchen.

Her mother gave her a reproving look. 'You've just had breakfast,' she said, following her daughter inside. 'You don't need another drink.'

'But I'm thirsty,' protested Amy, and Matt opened the fridge and pulled out a can of cola.

'Help yourself,' he said, taking a glass from the cupboard.

He hoped it would give him a chance to have a private word with Fliss. He arched his brows in her direction and they moved to the far side of the room. 'Everything OK?'

'As it will ever be, I suppose,' she said tightly, shedding her own backpack, and he found himself staring at her breasts again.

Dragging his eyes away, he said the first thing that came into his head. 'Your father doesn't approve of me, does he?'

'He doesn't know you.'

'Nor do you.'

She averted her eyes. 'I know enough.'

'You think?'

She looked at him then. 'Are you trying to get out of this arrangement?'

'No.'

She shook her head, and her hair, which was loose about her shoulders this morning, fell forward to hide her face. 'Maybe you should.'

Her drooping stance made him long to put out his hand and loop that fiery curtain back behind her ear so he could see her expression. But with Amy watching them over the rim of her glass, he restrained himself.

All the same, he was aware that spending time with Fliss was probably not the most sensible thing he'd done in his life. She disturbed him in ways Diane never had, and, although she was not conventionally beautiful, her creamy features had a warmth and sensuality that was far sexier than mere good looks could ever be.

Strictly speaking, he supposed, trying to downplay his attraction, she was slightly overweight. Her breasts were full, possibly too full, and the generous swell of her hips gave a distinctly provocative curve to her bottom. Yet in low-rise pink cut-offs, with white daisies hand-embroidered along the seams, and a matching cropped T-shirt that exposed her navel, she reminded him of things that, in his condition, were better forgotten.

'What's wrong?'

Predictably, Amy broke the uneasy silence that had fallen, and Matt realised that it was up to him to rescue the situation.

'Nothing's wrong,' he assured her lightly. 'I'll get my shoes.'

Although he thought about changing his shorts for jeans, it seemed a pointless exercise. It wasn't as if by changing his clothes he was going to change his feelings towards Fliss, and she was unlikely to be impressed by his judgement, either way.

By the time he came back downstairs, Fliss had washed up Amy's glass and his breakfast dishes, but he still couldn't say how she really felt about this outing. It was obvious she hadn't wanted to disappoint Amy, but taking him along…

That had definitely been an afterthought.

He backed the four-by-four out of the garage and indicated that they should get in while he locked up the house. But, as he was closing the front door, the phone rang.

Cursing, he opened the door again and was about to answer it when it occurred to him that it might be Diane. It was the weekend, after all. Perhaps she'd expected him to invite her down for a visit.

He closed the door again, inserting his key in the lock with grim determination. He didn't have time to talk to her, he told himself firmly, ignoring the fact that he owed her a call. Then, picking up the sports bag containing a towel and a six-pack of diet cola, he ran down the steps to where the Land Cruiser was waiting.

He'd half expected Fliss to put Amy in the front. Anything to avoid another loaded conversation with him. But common sense had prevailed, and Amy was seated in the back of the vehicle, her seat-belt fastened firmly across her lap.

Fliss glanced at him curiously as he got into the driving seat beside her. 'Wasn't that your phone?'

He didn't look at her as he started the car. 'So?'

'So—oughtn't you to have answered it?'

Matt's mouth compressed. 'Probably,' he agreed carelessly, putting the heavy vehicle into gear and turning down the drive. 'Where are we going?'

He was aware of Fliss giving him a studied look, but it was Amy who answered him. 'We usually go to Cobbleton,' she said, leaning forward to tap her mother on the shoulder. 'Isn't that right, Mum?'

Fliss shrugged. 'Maybe Mr Quinn would prefer to go somewhere else,' she replied, that prim note of disapproval Matt found most challenging in her voice.

'I don't know this area at all,' he declared, glancing over his shoulder at his other passenger. 'But Cobbleton sounds good to me. You'll have to give me directions how to get there.'

'Oh—' Amy put a finger to her lips. 'Well, I know it's not that far.' She paused. 'Perhaps Mummy could tell you which way to go. She knows, don't you, Mum?'

He heard Fliss give a small sigh. 'I'm sure Mr Quinn would rather go somewhere he knows,' she said stiffly. 'He's not that unfamiliar with the area. His fiancée's parents live in the village.'

'What's a fiancée?' asked Amy innocently before Matt could reply, and Fliss turned to give her daughter a tight smile.

'That needn't concern you—'

'I don't have a fiancée,' Matt overrode her grimly, and then, as they reached the crossroads on the outskirts of the village, 'Which way?'

'Cobbleton is that way.'

Fliss waved a dismissive hand in the direction she wanted him to take, but he could feel the censure oozing from her pores. It annoyed the hell out of him. Dammit, the reason why he hadn't answered his phone was nothing to do with her. Because that was what this was all about. He just knew it. Did she suspect it might have been Diane? Of course she did. But why the hell did she care what Diane thought when the other woman clearly had no such inhibitions about her?

For a while they travelled in silence. A signpost at the next junction offered the information that Lyme Regis and Honiton were in one direction, while Brightsea and Cobbleton were in the other, so there was no argument over which road to take.

Even Amy had subsided into silence, and he guessed his angry outburst had frightened her a little.

That annoyed him more than it should. He and Amy had got along so well up to that point, and he didn't like to think that she blamed herself for his attitude towards her mother.

Taking a deep breath, he glanced over his shoulder again and said pleasantly, 'Tell me about Cobbleton. I've never heard of it. I guess it isn't a big place.'

Amy hesitated, but shyness was not her strong suit. 'No, it's just small,' she agreed. 'But we like it, don't we, Mum? We've been lots of times.'

'Sounds good.' Matt concentrated on the road, determinedly not looking at Fliss. If she wanted to sulk, that was her problem. 'Does it get many visitors?'

'Some,' said Amy thoughtfully. 'But we don't bother with them. We use'ly just go down to the beach, don't we, Mum?'

Fliss gave a noncommittal shrug and Matt stifled an oath. This was going to be some outing if she refused to speak unless she was spoken to. Dammit, couldn't she see that he was making an effort here?

'Do you swim?' he asked now, looking deliberately at her, and Fliss was obliged to acknowledge his question.

'You can, if you want to.'

'That's not what I asked.'

She shifted a little uncomfortably in her seat. 'Not if Amy and I are on our own,' she replied unwillingly. 'She can swim, but the beach drops away quite steeply once you're in the water. I'd be afraid she'd get into difficulties and I couldn't get to her.'

'Right.' Matt was grateful to have got more than a monosyllabic answer at last. 'So—are there no lifeguards?'

Fliss gave him an incredulous look. 'At Cobbleton? It's a fishing village, Mr Quinn. Not Bondi Beach!'

'It's Matt,' he said evenly. Then, 'There are lifeguards all over the place, not just on Bondi Beach.'

'Which I suppose you know all about,' said Fliss shortly, and he raised a modest eyebrow.

'That there are lifeguards all over the place?' he asked innocently. 'Oh, yeah, I—'

'I meant Bondi Beach,' she corrected him, even though Matt was fairly sure she'd known exactly what he was doing. 'I expect you've travelled all over the world.'

'Well, not all,' he said mildly. 'But I have been to Oz. Have you?'

Fliss snorted in disbelief, but once again it was Amy who intervened. 'What's Oz?'

'Australia,' said Matt and Fliss in unison, and then she exchanged a reluctant smile with him. 'People call it Oz because it's easier to say than Australia,' he added for the child's benefit, giving her mother a conciliatory look. 'Bondi Beach is a famous Australian landmark.'

'Oh.'

As Amy absorbed this information, Matt tried again with Fliss. 'I don't know what Diane's told you, but she and I are not engaged. We never have been. Chances are we never will be.'

'Well, it's nothing to do with me,' she said, turning to look out of the window, and for some reason that really annoyed him.

'Yeah, right,' he muttered. 'That's why you've taken a vow of silence, is it? Or was it because I didn't answer my phone? Forgive me, but I thought that was my business, not yours.'

Of course that was unforgivable and he knew it. He didn't need to see the hectic colour that stained her cheeks to know he'd offended her again, and he swore under his breath.

'Do you want to go back?' he demanded, deciding he was too tired of fighting off his own demons to contemplate fighting hers, too. Either she wanted to spend the day with him or she didn't. It was her call.

She said nothing for a few moments and he was already looking for somewhere to turn the car when she said in a low voice, 'Do you?'

Matt did a double take. 'Me?'

'Yes, you,' she murmured unhappily. 'You're right. What

you do is not my concern. I had no right to interfere. Particularly as you've been kind enough to offer to take us to the beach.'

Matt shook his head. 'Don't say that.' And when she looked uncomprehendingly at him, he continued, 'It wasn't kind at all. I gatecrashed your outing with Amy, and I'm guessing your father wouldn't have suddenly acquired a use for his car if I hadn't been coming along.'

'You could be right.' Fliss cast a nervous glance over her shoulder as she answered him, but Matt could see Amy in his rear-view mirror and she didn't appear to be listening to them. 'I'm sorry.'

'Hey, I'm used to it.' Matt grimaced. 'The Press went from hanging on every word I spoke when I got back, to writing eulogies about my mental incompetence when I began refusing interviews.'

Fliss looked at him then. 'Are you saying they wrote lies about you?'

Matt pulled a wry face. 'Nothing libellous, I don't think. They have teams of legal experts who pore over every word that's printed to ensure they don't have to pay out a fortune in damages.'

'Then—'

'You have to understand that not everything you read is gospel. So long as there's a germ of truth in there somewhere they can argue that they're justified in reporting the story.' He paused and then went on doggedly. 'Like the fact that I was— well, for want of a better word, traumatised when I got back. That provided endless columns of newsprint, I can tell you.'

Fliss frowned. 'But being traumatised doesn't mean you're mentally incompetent.'

'No.' Matt sighed, his hands tightening on the leather steering wheel. 'But it could be argued that it depends on the degree of trauma, and most people reading the article would accept that. Hell, I'd have accepted it myself if I hadn't had firsthand experience of that kind of grey journalism.'

He saw her bite her lip, and the tightening in his groin caught him unawares. This wasn't what he'd had in mind when he offered to take them to the beach, and it was unsettling to find that she still had that effect on him.

'But you were—traumatised,' she said at last, looking down at her hands. 'Weren't you?'

Matt expelled a weary breath, and told himself he was glad her words had dispelled his moment of madness. 'Oh, yeah,' he said flatly. 'Traumatised, right. A pitiful excuse for a man, that's what I was when I got back.'

Fliss glanced at him. 'It must have been a terrible experience.'

'Yeah.' Matt conceded the point, and then, because he needed someone to understand his dilemma, he went on, 'It was all my own fault, really. I wanted a story and I suppose I never thought they'd imagine I might be a spy.' He grimaced. 'Me? A spy? How ludicrous can you get?'

'Oh, I don't know.' Fliss regarded him thoughtfully. 'I thought you looked—well, different, when I first saw you.'

'Different?' He was wary.

'Sort of—dangerous,' she admitted unwillingly. 'It's your haircut, I think. It's very short.'

'Ah.' Matt raked his nails over his scalp, absorbing that confession. It was kind of reassuring to know he didn't look like the wimp he felt. 'Anyway, that was their excuse for taking me prisoner. And, when I couldn't answer their questions, they—got angry.'

Fliss glanced at Amy then, but he knew she knew exactly what he meant. And he found to his amazement that it was liberating to talk about it. It didn't seem half so terrifying when he was discussing it with her.

'So—how did you get away?' she asked, and he sensed her nervousness in asking the question. After all, if she'd read anything about him she'd know that he'd never discussed his experiences publicly.

'One of the rebel captains arranged for a Jeep to be waiting for me,' he said. And then, with an effort, 'He saved me from a fate worse than death, if you know what I mean.'

'My God!' Fliss stared at him for a moment, and then put out her hand and touched his knee. 'I'm sorry. No wonder you were traumatised when you got home.'

'What's traum'tised?' asked Amy, leaning forward, and Matt wondered how much she'd heard or understood. Not a lot, he guessed, and he was so grateful to Fliss for listening to him and understanding. He had the feeling no other woman of his acquaintance would have reacted so positively to his story.

'Traumatised means depressed,' Fliss said now, glancing at Matt again for his approval. 'Mr Quinn was just telling me about someone who had lies written about them because they were ill.'

'Really?'

Amy sounded only mildly interested, and Matt gave her mother a rueful smile. 'Thanks,' he said. 'For that and for not judging me.' He blew out a breath. 'So—how much further do we have to go?'

Despite its inauspicious beginnings, it was a good day. Matt, who had started out feeling tense and irritable, found himself relaxing completely. Amy had that kind of effect on him, and although Fliss caused a different reaction entirely their combined companionship was exactly what he needed.

With Amy, he could forget everything but how easy it was to please a child, and because she was there, his relationship with Fliss couldn't progress in a way that might have embarrassed both of them. Amy made him wish he had a child of his own, a possibility that seemed exceedingly remote now, but at least he could pretend she was his. And there was no doubt that anyone seeing the three of them together would assume she was.

As Amy had said, Cobbleton was little more than a village on Lyme Bay. A small harbour gave refuge to the handful of fishing boats that still used this stretch of the coast as a mooring, but its main attraction was the unspoilt spread of beach that curved away from the river estuary. Fliss said that the muddy flats to the west of the harbour were rich in bird life, and Matt thought how different it was from the arid sand-dunes that had rolled back from the coast in Abuqara.

After leaving the Land Cruiser on the quay, they spent some time exploring the rocks that edged the harbour. Amy was fascinated by the crabs and other crustaceans Matt turned up, and even Fliss took off her tennis shoes and paddled in the shallows.

Then they climbed back up onto the quay and followed the narrow promenade along to where the seemingly miles of unblemished sand stretched away to limestone cliffs. It was getting hotter all the time as the sun rose higher in the sky and they were all glad to relax for a while on the rug Fliss pulled from her backpack.

If Matt was intensely conscious of Fliss's slim limbs only inches from the hairy length of his up-drawn knee, he tried not to think about it. But there was no denying that he was conscious of her with every fibre of his being, and only Amy's presence prevented him from doing something totally outrageous like testing the shape of her calf with his hand. The memory of how she had looked in his dream two nights ago hadn't gone away and he wondered if he was doomed to spend the rest of his life hankering after something he could never have. If so, it was going to be a pretty miserable existence, and when Amy suggested that they ought to cool off in the water he was more than willing to oblige.

It was only when she started stripping off her shorts and T-shirt that he realised she didn't just mean that they should go paddling. She was wearing a pretty blue-flowered bikini beneath her clothes and she obviously expected him to accompany her.

Fliss, perhaps sensing his ambivalence, said quickly, 'Don't go out of your depth, Amy,' and the little girl pulled a disappointed face.

'I can swim, Mum,' she protested, but Fliss was adamant.

'I mean it, Amy. I don't want to have to come into the water after you. Unlike you, I haven't brought my swimsuit.'

For a moment, Matt allowed himself to entertain an erotic

image of Fliss racing stark naked into the sea. But such images were not productive, even if they did have the desirable side-effect of propelling him to his feet.

'I'll go with her,' he said, forgetting for a moment that by hauling off his shirt he was exposing his scarred back to public gaze. There were few people on the beach, it was true, but if anybody did notice him they were bound to be curious as to where he'd got his injuries. Still, what the hell? he thought grimly. He couldn't spend the rest of his days hiding from life.

He'd reckoned without Amy, of course, and, although they walked down to the sea together, as soon as he plunged into the waves she was given an unrivalled view of his back. For a few moments he was intent on acclimatising his body heat to the much cooler temperature of the water, but when he turned onto his back and looked towards the shore he found the little girl still standing in the shallows where he'd left her.

'Are you coming in?' he called, but Amy only stood there shaking her head and he realised she was upset.

Raking back his short hair with a careless hand, he wondered what was the matter. Whatever, he knew he would have to do something about it. At any moment, Fliss was going to notice something was wrong. If Amy was upset about his injuries this was something he and the child had to deal with together.

He was still within his depth and, standing up, he waded back to the shallows, shivering a little in spite of the heat of the sun. 'What's wrong?'

Amy sniffed. 'I don't want to go swimming,' she said off-handedly. 'I'm going back to Mummy.'

'Wait!' Matt had no experience in these matters, but something told him he could do this. 'Is it me that's upset you?'

'No.'

But Amy wouldn't look at him and he knew it was. 'Is it the scars on my back?' he persisted gently.

'No.' Amy flicked him an indignant look. 'I just don't feel like swimming anymore.'

'OK.' Matt lifted his shoulders in a careless gesture. 'I'll have to swim on my own, then.'

Amy pursed her lips. 'All right.'

'All right.'

Matt turned away, but before he'd taken more than a few steps Amy spoke again. 'What happened to your back? Did you have an accident?'

His shoulders rounded now, but he turned back again. 'No. It's like I told your mummy. The people who put me in prison thought I was a bad man so they—punished me.'

Amy's eyes widened. 'Does it hurt?'

'Not anymore.'

She caught her breath. 'They must be really bad men.'

'I suppose that depends on your point of view.'

He gave her a rueful smile. 'I'd been warned not to go too far from my hotel in Abuqara City, but I thought I'd be clever and get an interview with this old mullah—er, man—who was believed to have contact with the rebel forces. He did, and by the time I realised how stupid I'd been it was too late.'

'Too late for what?'

'I think that's enough, Amy,' murmured a soft voice close by and Matt realised that, in concentrating on the little girl, he'd missed the fact that Fliss had come to join them. She was looking at him now with that mixture of regret and understanding in her eyes he'd seen before, and he wondered why he found it so easy to talk to her and her daughter when it was so difficult for him to talk to anyone else.

CHAPTER ELEVEN

THEY drove back to Mallon's End in the late afternoon. Amy was tired, and Fliss wasn't surprised when she glanced over her shoulder to find the little girl had fallen asleep. It had been a long day for her, filled with activity, and Fliss wished she knew how to thank Matt for his kindness towards her daughter.

Matt himself seemed quite willing to remain silent on the return journey, but it was an amicable silence, much different from the charged atmosphere she had created that morning. But, dammit, Diane had said he was her fiancé, Fliss defended herself. And she was fairly sure that was who Matt had suspected was on the phone.

However, that was nothing to do with her, and the fact that Matt had confided in her about his experiences had been much more important. Her skin tingled just thinking about what he'd had to go through, and she suspected that if Amy hadn't been there, her attraction to him might well have got her into other difficulties. There was no doubt there had been times when the tension between them had been almost palpable.

Not least when she'd interrupted his conversation with Amy at the water's edge early in the day. Just remembering how he'd looked then, all dark and tanned and wet, made her feel shivery. His cargo shorts had been clinging to his legs, outlining every bulge that they were supposed to cover. He'd have looked less sexy if he'd been naked, she thought ruefully, her pulse quickening in spite of herself. Although perhaps not. She knew better than anyone that Matt always looked sexy, with or without his clothes.

Still, she was glad she hadn't taken her swimsuit with her. Her bikini, which she'd had for far too many years, would only have accentuated the extra pounds she'd put on since Amy was

119

born. She could just imagine how she'd have looked, her breasts spilling out of the cups of the bra, the bikini briefs tight around her hips. Oh, yes, she was no photographic model, nor ever would be.

Later in the morning, they'd all played beach cricket before retiring to the fast-food restaurant that adjoined the harbour. Fliss had brought sandwiches for lunch, but Matt's offer of cheeseburger and chips and a delicious cup of freshly brewed coffee had been too tempting to turn down. Which would have done little for her waistline, she acknowledged now. But what the hell? She wasn't trying to impress anyone.

After lunch, they'd gone for a walk along the cliffs, and Matt had entertained Amy by telling her stories of the pirate ships that had used to patrol the coastline on the lookout for young women they sold into slavery in North Africa.

'Like you were?' Amy had asked artlessly, and Matt had exchanged a wry look with Fliss before saying flatly, 'In a manner of speaking.' But Fliss had been left with the impression that that was one aspect of his captivity he still found hard to discuss.

It was just after five o'clock when they reached the village, but, although Fliss had expected Matt to drop her and Amy at the cottage, he drove directly to the Old Coaching House.

'Amy's still asleep,' he said, glancing significantly into the back of the vehicle. 'It seems a shame to wake her.'

It did, but Fliss was sure that when the engine was switched off Amy would wake up. However, even after Matt had parked the four-by-four on the forecourt, her daughter still slept on, and he made a silent indication that they should go inside.

'She'll be OK,' he said in a low voice when Fliss looked as if she might argue. 'She'll come and find us when she's ready.'

Fliss guessed she would, but she had certain misgivings about going into the house with him. Which was ridiculous really, considering she spent hours alone with him when she was working. But somehow that was different.

He left the front door ajar so that Amy would know at once where they were and then led the way into the newly furnished drawing room. Here, a pair of squashy leather sofas faced one another across the hearth, and Matt had installed an entertainment centre in a carved mahogany cabinet. The oversized furniture suited the spacious, high-ceilinged room, and Fliss couldn't help admiring her own handiwork in the polish that gleamed on every wooden surface. The extravagant arrangement of ferns and lilies that occupied an end table was her doing, too. She'd rescued the blossoms from the weed-choked garden, and she remembered suddenly that she still hadn't asked Matt if he intended to hire a gardener.

'Sit down,' he said now, indicating one of the sofas, disappearing out the door again before she could answer him.

But Fliss was too much on edge to relax. Instead, she drifted over to the windows, peering out for a minute before a glimpse of her reflection in one of the long mirrors that hung beside the fireplace caught her attention.

She stared in disgust at the image that confronted her. She might not go brown but her skin did burn easily, and right now her face was as red as a tomato. It clashed vividly with her hair, and with the delicate pink of her T-shirt and trousers. Which only added to the feelings of inadequacy that had plagued her on the way home.

She was still staring broodingly at her reflection when Matt's image appeared behind her. He'd evidently dumped the sports bag that had contained his towel but he hadn't yet changed his clothes.

Though why should he? she thought bitterly. Even in creased shorts he looked like a big, sleek cat, watchful and vaguely predatory.

Fliss would have moved away from the mirror then but his solid bulk behind her prevented a graceful retreat. Besides, there was no point in pretending she hadn't been looking at herself. He already knew she had.

Something of how she was feeling must have shown in her expression, because he said, 'What's wrong?' in a rough, sympathetic tone that made her want to confide in him.

'Need you ask?' she cried, indicating her face. 'Why didn't you tell me?'

'What? That you look as if you've had a fun day in the sun?' he asked gently. His warm breath stirred the hair at her nape. 'Stop beating up on yourself. You look OK to me.'

'That's because you're not looking at me like—like a man looks at a woman,' she retorted, wondering if she'd have been as brave if she'd been facing him. Talking to his mirror image was different somehow, although his sudden scowl did make her wish she hadn't said anything.

'How am I looking at you?' he asked now in a dangerously soft voice, and she shifted a little uneasily beneath his narrow-eyed gaze.

'You know,' she protested helplessly. Then, because he was evidently expecting something more, 'I think you like me but—well, you're not attracted to me.'

'And you know this how?'

'Oh…' She shook her head, but, when she would have moved away from the mirror, his hand on her shoulder kept her where she was. She sighed. 'Does it matter?' Then, the lie almost sticking in her throat, 'Anyway, I'm not attracted to you either.'

'No?'

Oh, God, had he sensed how she was feeling? 'No!'

'I see.'

He seemed to be digesting this, but he didn't remove his hand from her shoulder. Instead she watched, transfixed, as one finger probed the scooped neckline of her shirt while his other hand curved almost experimentally about her bare midriff.

Everywhere he touched her skin bloomed with heat, competing with her hot face for precedence. His hands were cool and dry, but they burned her flesh, setting off tiny electric shocks throughout her body.

Through the haze of need he was inspiring in her, Fliss managed to find her voice. 'Why don't you go and get changed?' she said, hoping he would take the hint and stop tormenting her. Because that was what he was doing. She was sure of it.

This was his way of proving that she'd been lying when she'd said she wasn't attracted to him.

'Why?' he asked, dipping his head so that she was forced to meet his eyes in the mirror. 'Do I smell?'

Oh, yeah. Fliss swallowed the catch in her throat. He smelled of salt and warmth and sun-dried skin overlaid with a tantalising aroma of raw male virility. The man was testosterone on legs and he must know it.

'Look, perhaps I ought to go and wake Amy,' she said, hoping the introduction of her daughter's name might bring a touch of sanity to the proceedings. 'She'll never sleep tonight.'

'Nor will I,' said Matt in that low, hoarse voice that never failed to stir her senses. He moved his head and the scratch of stubble on his jawline grazed her neck. 'But don't let that worry you.'

Fliss's whole body felt hot now, hot and alive and pulsing with need. When his hips brushed against hers, she felt an urgent desire to push herself against him. But what would she do if she discovered he was as aroused as she was? She had no experience in playing the seductress.

In any case, it would never happen, she assured herself grimly. Whatever game he was playing, he would never let it go that far. Teasing her, tempting her, that was his objective. He wanted her to know what she was missing in her life. As if she didn't know that already.

Then his tongue traced the taut cord in her neck below her ear, following it down to where it expanded to meet her shoulder, and her stomach contracted. Standing in front of the mirror, she could see clearly what he was doing, and, when his lids lifted so that she could see his eyes, her breath caught in her throat.

'Wh—why are you doing this?'

Matt's tongue circled his lips for a moment before replying. 'Don't you like it?' he asked huskily, and Fliss thought no woman in her right mind would say no.

'That's—not the point,' she said, watching him as his fingers splayed possessively over her stomach, his thumb probing the sensitive hollow of her navel. 'You—you shouldn't.'

'Probably not,' he agreed after a moment, his voice muffled as his lips replaced his tongue. 'But you sure do taste good. I'd forgotten how good a real woman could taste.'

Yeah, right. Fliss didn't believe that for a moment. Whatever lies Diane may have told about their relationship, she was still involved with him. It had been obvious from her attitude that she considered him her property, and the reason for that wasn't hard to understand.

'Matt, please…' Fliss whispered now, hardly recognising the pleading tone of her own voice. She sounded almost wanton, she thought, all yielding allure and sensual appeal. Whatever guilt she felt about Diane, she wasn't above ignoring it if it suited her. But, heaven help her, this was never likely to happen to her again.

The urge to tip her head back against his shoulder was almost irresistible. He was so close, she could feel the heat coming off his body in waves. She would have had to be totally numb to remain immune to it, and because her eyes were continually drawn to the mirror, she could view what Matt was doing to her with a curious detachment.

Not that that made it any less erotic. When Matt's eyes met hers again, she felt as if her breathing had been suspended. Still watching her, he deliberately bit her neck and drew the soft flesh into his mouth. Sucking on it greedily, he continued to impale her with his gaze.

His action inflamed Fliss's senses and her knees wobbled. Dear God, did he realise what he was doing to her? Did he know she was finding it very hard to stay in control? His hand had left her shoulder now and was sliding seductively over her ribcage. His knuckles grazed her nipple, causing another debilitating surge of heat, and she fought back the moan of pleasure that threatened to betray her.

Her breasts were tingling, both nipples clearly defined against her cotton shirt. She was wearing a bra, but its lacy cups offered little protection, and when Matt's eyes were drawn to them wetness pooled between her legs.

Her eyes closed almost instinctively. She'd had no experience of Matt's kind of lovemaking and she didn't want to see she was making a complete fool of herself. He hadn't even kissed her yet and she was already anticipating how that would feel. She wanted—oh, lord, she didn't know exactly what she wanted. But the image of Matt's bed with its tumbled sheets went some way to supplying an answer.

'Open your eyes,' he said, his mouth against her ear, and her lids lifted obediently. 'That's better,' he murmured, the tips of his fingers slipping beneath the hem of her T-shirt. 'It's more fun if you're watching me.'

Fun? Fliss sucked in a breath. Is that what he thought this was? Didn't he know that every nerve in her body was screaming with need?

There were daisy buttons on the front of her trousers instead of a zip and her breathing suspended completely when Matt changed direction, his fingers tiptoeing from one button to the other on a direct path to her crotch. He didn't open the buttons. He didn't have to. Fliss was ahead of him, and when he reached the junction of her legs and cupped her in his hand, she almost climaxed there and then.

But it couldn't go on. If Amy woke up and came looking for them… Well, that didn't bear thinking about. Grabbing his hand with both of hers, she pushed it away.

'Don't,' she said abruptly. 'We can't do this.'

'Can't we?' He lifted his head and regarded her with dark enquiry. 'I thought we were.'

'You don't understand. Amy could wake up.'

'I know that.'

'Well, then…'

'Let me worry about Amy.'

'No.' She swallowed. 'This is wrong.'

'Is it?' He was mocking now. 'You seemed to be enjoying it a moment ago.'

'Matt!'

'Fliss!' He mimicked her breathless denial. 'Stop stressing. We're not hurting anyone.'

'How can you say that?'

She turned her head to stare at him and then wished she hadn't when she found they were face to face. His mouth was only inches from hers, and before she could turn away again he moved closer and covered her lips with his.

It wasn't like the other time she'd kissed him. Then, she'd been intensely aware that it was she who was making the running. This time Matt himself had initiated the contact. And because her lips were still parted in surprise, it was a wet and open-mouthed meeting of lips and tongues.

His mouth was soft, but incredibly hot, his tongue a sensual invasion she had no will to resist. Finding him this close to her, breathing his breath, feeling his heat, was a mindless pleasure. The images she'd had before were overlaid with other visions now, of naked bodies and thrashing limbs, of her and Matt in bed together. Anticipating how satisfying that would be, to have him not only in her arms but *inside* her, implied an awesome intimacy. And was far too devastating to ignore.

She tried to turn fully towards him, but he wouldn't let her, and she could only clutch at his shirt with both hands. Simple lust was roaring through her veins, leaving her eager, yet helpless, and for several minutes she was held captive by her own body's demands.

His mouth left hers at last and she wanted to howl in protest. But he turned her back towards the mirror and buried his face in the hollow of her neck. She sensed he was fighting his own needs; aware that with every minute that passed Amy was more likely to interrupt them. It was a sobering thought and it made her feel better knowing that he was frustrated by it, too.

And then her reflection intruded. She hardly recognised herself now. Her cheeks were still burned, but the flush extended down her throat as well. Her mouth looked swollen and there was a distinct mark on her neck where Matt had bitten her. Oh, God, she thought in horror, how on earth was she going to explain that?

Amy would notice immediately, she thought. Her daughter always noticed everything, whether Fliss wanted her to or not. And if she mentioned it to her grandfather...

The sound of the phone brought an end to any further speculation. Brought an end to Matt's sensuous exploration of her shoulder, too, and he lifted his head reluctantly and met her anxious gaze in the glass.

'What's the matter?'

Immediately he'd sensed her feelings, and with a determined effort she pulled away. 'Your phone's ringing.'

'Yeah. I hear it.'

Fliss pressed her lips together. She was not going to tell him he should answer it, she assured herself firmly, but something of her ambivalence must have shown in her eyes because he said a little tensely, 'What? What?'

'Nothing,' she murmured, suddenly noticing that the top button on her trousers was undone. When had that happened? she wondered, hastily fastening it again. 'Um—I'd better go and collect Amy. It's getting late.'

'Something's wrong,' said Matt doggedly. 'I knew that before that bloody thing started ringing.' He cut a scowling glance towards the hall. 'Stop, can't you?'

The unexpected cessation of sound was almost deafening and Fliss ran a nervous hand over her midriff. Then, reminded of how Matt had done the same, she stuffed her hands into her pockets instead. 'That's a relief,' she said, hoping to avoid another argument. 'You must have supernatural powers.'

'Though not with you, huh?' he countered flatly. He waited and, when she didn't answer him, he said, 'Have you stopped speaking to me again?'

Fliss sighed. 'Of course not.'

'So what's bugging you?'

'You mean other than the fact that I should have had more sense than to go along with this?' she demanded flippantly, but he wasn't amused.

'You're saying what we did was against your will?'

'No—'

'Gee, thanks.'

'But we both know you were only amusing yourself at my expense.'

'Do we?'

Fliss made an exasperated sound. 'Do I look like I was born yesterday?'

'And your point is?'

'Look at me, Matt. Really look at me. Then tell me you don't know what I'm talking about. I may be amusing, but I'm certainly not the kind of woman that men like—that men are irresistibly attracted to.'

'Men like me, you mean? Don't underestimate yourself.'

'And don't you underestimate me,' she retorted hotly. 'What happened here—well, it was quite an experience. But Diane will soon come here—'

'Leave Diane out of this,' he snapped, but she wouldn't back down.

'That's really what this is all about,' she went on unsteadily. 'You've had a row with her—probably over you moving down here—and you decided to give your housekeeper a thrill.'

Matt looked appalled. 'Do you believe that? Is that what you really think of me?'

It wasn't, but Fliss consoled herself with the thought that his ego was probably much less vulnerable than hers.

'Does it matter what I think?' she asked wearily. Then, as the phone started to ring again, she made a defeated gesture. 'Go on. Answer it. She's not going to give up until you do.'

CHAPTER TWELVE

AMY was grumpy on the walk back to the cottage. She hadn't taken kindly to being woken up and she didn't understand why she couldn't go into the house and speak to Matt before they went home.

'But I haven't said bye-bye,' she protested, when her mother announced that they were leaving right away. 'Can't I just go and thank him for coming with us? It wouldn't have been half as much fun if he hadn't.'

Well, thanks, thought Fliss drily, but she had more important things on her mind. 'Not today,' she insisted crisply, marching her daughter firmly along the path towards the churchyard gate. 'In any case, he's busy. The phone rang and—he went to answer it.'

Which might or might not be a lie, she conceded as Amy squirmed impatiently out of her grasp. Whether Matt had answered the call or not wasn't her business. Either way, it was an excuse Amy could identify with.

Unfortunately, the little girl chose to turn her disappointment on her mother and, noticing Fliss's hot face, she said, 'Why are you all red? Did you and Matt have another argument? Is that why I'm not allowed to speak to him?'

'No!' Fliss was horrified at the suggestion. But she had to admit that Amy was getting far too astute for her own good. 'In case you overlooked the fact, it's been a sunny day. I'm sunburned, that's all.'

'So why aren't I sunburned?' Amy countered, still regarding her mother's face with curious eyes. Then she gasped. 'Did you know you've got a big bruise on your neck, as well?'

Fliss's hand went automatically to cover the mark Matt had made, and she was glad her face couldn't look any redder than it already did. 'Oh—I must have been bitten,' she said, cringing at the irony. 'That's why I get sunburned and you don't. My skin is much fairer than yours.'

'Really?' Amy didn't look convinced and, despite Fliss's efforts to distract her, she still kept casting curious looks at her mother whenever she thought she could get away with it.

'Yes, really,' declared Fliss at last, feeling as if her nerves had been strung out to dry. Then, because she couldn't let Amy waltz into the cottage with the news that her mother had been bitten by some monstrous insect, she said, 'And I'd prefer it if you didn't tell Grandad.'

'Why?'

Why? Fliss stifled the sob of hysteria that rose in her throat. How was she supposed to answer that? 'Well—well, because we don't want to worry him, do we?' And that was the truth. She took a breath and then continued firmly, 'You know he wasn't very keen on us going out today. We don't want to give him anything else to—to—'

'To complain about?' suggested Amy shrewdly, and Fliss reflected that her daughter was growing up fast.

'Sort of,' she said now, not wanting to feel guilty about her father, too. 'And we have had a lovely day, haven't we?'

'Oh, yes.' Amy nodded. 'I really like Quinn, don't you?'

'Mr Quinn,' Fliss corrected her swiftly, and Amy pulled a face.

'You call him Matt.'

'I don't.'

'You do. I heard you tell Grandad that it was me who let Harvey into Matt's garden.'

'You hear too much!' exclaimed Fliss shortly. 'Anyway, that doesn't matter now.' She took a breath. 'So, we're agreed? We won't say anything to Grandad about my—bite.'

'OK.'

Amy gave a dismissive shrug of her shoulders and Fliss had to be content with that. In any case, they'd reached the far side of the churchyard now, and it would only take them another minute to reach the cottage. No more time to coach her daughter, no more time to prepare herself for her father's interrogation.

But, in the event, George Taylor wasn't at home. Although the Fiesta was parked on the short drive, both he and Harvey were absent. Fliss guessed he'd taken the dog for a walk and would probably be calling in at the pub for a drink before coming home. It gave her the opportunity to go and take a shower and change her clothes before he came in.

It occurred to her that the reason the car had been left on the drive was that her father expected her to go to the supermarket in Westerbury when she got back. But the shopping would have to wait, she decided. There was always tomorrow and she really wanted to get out of these clothes.

In consequence, Amy was sprawled on the sofa in the living room watching television and Fliss was stirring a pan of bolognaise at the stove when her father and Harvey returned.

As usual, Harvey took the edge off any atmosphere that still lingered, and, determined not to bear a grudge, Fliss greeted her father with a cheerful smile. 'Supper's almost ready.'

'Good.'

If there was still a note of hostility in his voice, Fliss chose to ignore it. Instead she ran a surreptitious hand around the neckline of her high-necked sweater, assuring herself that the mark Matt had left couldn't be seen. Then, turning back to the table, she placed two wine glasses beside their plates. 'I thought I'd open a bottle of that claret Patrick sent you,' she went on, trying to act as if they hadn't had that unpleasant contretemps that morning. Then, when he didn't respond, 'Have you had a nice day?'

She heard him suck in a breath. 'Do you care?' he enquired at last, and Fliss turned back to the hob to hide her resigned expression.

'Of course I care.'

'But not enough to give up any invitation that comes your way,' he retorted. 'Despite the fact that I expressed my disapproval of this particular relationship.'

Fliss sighed. 'I have to make my own decisions, Dad,'

she said evenly. She hesitated. 'I like Mr Quinn. And so does Amy.'

Her father snorted. 'And that settles it, does it? You know next to nothing about this man, Felicity. Why would you consider his opinion more important than mine?'

Fliss gasped, turning to face him again. 'You're being unreasonable, Dad,' she said. 'I'm not having an affair with him, for heaven's sake!' Though she'd come damn close to it, she had to admit. 'We're—friends, that's all. What on earth is wrong with that?'

'You do know he's engaged to Diane Chesney, don't you?'

'He's not!'

Now, why had she said that?

'He denied it, I gather?' George Taylor's lips curled scornfully. 'I have to ask myself in what circumstances such an intimate confidence would be expressed.'

Fliss pressed her lips together, but she couldn't let him go on thinking the worst. 'The phone started ringing as we were leaving,' she said defensively. 'I said it was probably his fiancée and he said—he said he didn't have a fiancée.'

'And you believed him, of course?'

Fliss shook her head. 'You're going to make something of it whatever I say,' she replied flatly. She didn't like to think what he'd say if he ever found out what they'd been doing since they got back. 'Amy!' She called the little girl's name to put an end to the discussion, and to distract her own thoughts from how devastatingly sensual Matt's kiss had been. 'Come and get your supper. It's ready.'

The meal smelled delicious, and no doubt it tasted that way, too, but Fliss couldn't enjoy it. Tension simmered around the table—and not just the tension of knowing that her father didn't approve of Matt, either. She also lived in fear of Amy saying something she shouldn't, and it didn't help when her father started asking the child how she'd enjoyed her day.

It was a sneaky way of finding out what they'd done and Fliss hoped the look she gave her father conveyed what she thought of his methods. But Amy was only too happy to describe the outing in detail, telling her grandfather how Matt had taken her swimming and that they'd all gone to McDonald's for lunch.

'That must be why your mother's not eating her supper,' he commented pleasantly. 'She's not hungry.' He paused. 'Or perhaps she's too warm. I must say, a high-necked jumper and denim jeans do seem excessive for a warm evening like this.'

Fliss stiffened. 'I was cold,' she said quickly. 'You know what it's like if you've been sunburned. You feel chilly later on.'

'That's right,' chimed Amy, even though Fliss had hoped to divert her. 'Mummy got really sunburned. All down her—' She met her mother's warning stare and broke off awkwardly. 'I mean—all down her arms.'

George Taylor was not deceived, Fliss could tell. The glance he gave her confirmed he'd intercepted the look she'd directed at Amy. 'All down her arms, eh?' he said, half-maliciously. 'Did Mr Quinn get burned, too?'

'Oh, no, but he's got these awful marks on his back that he got when he was in prison!' Amy exclaimed, clearly deciding her mother couldn't object to her talking about Matt. 'I didn't like them at first, but he—'

'Amy!'

Her mother's angry use of her name silenced the child, but George Taylor wasn't half so easy to control. 'She was only being honest,' he said, leaning across the table and patting his granddaughter's hand. Then he looked at Fliss again. 'I hope you've put some cream on your arms. You know how sensitive your skin is.'

'I'll survive,' said Fliss shortly, swallowing a mouthful of wine before getting up to clear the dirty plates away. 'Does anyone want ice cream?'

'Yes, please,' said Amy at once, soon recovering her confidence, but George Taylor shook his head.

'I've had enough,' he said. 'I think I'll go and sit in the garden for a while. Come and join me when you're finished, Amy. I'd love to hear some more about your trip.'

* * *

On Monday morning Matt woke with a hangover, which was hardly surprising considering he'd drunk the best part of a bottle of single malt the night before.

But Sunday had been a bloody awful day. He'd woken before dawn, disgruntled and soaked in sweat, with the tangible remains of the erotic dream he'd been having still tingling in his groin. He was half-aroused, but he knew better than to imagine it meant anything in his present condition. Morning erections were a thing of the past and the sooner he accepted it the better.

It was easier said than done, however. Frustration didn't go away. It still ate at him like a terminal illness, polluting his confidence and screwing up his head. And his attempted seduction of Fliss the day before had only added to his depression.

For it was Fliss again who had destroyed his rest; Fliss, whose warm, expressive face and lush body had haunted his sleep. She'd been beside him this time, her fiery hair spread across his pillow, her white limbs entwined with his. Her full breasts had tantalised him, swollen and round beneath his hand. When he'd moved closer her legs had parted invitingly, and the tight curls that were all that barred his way were as fiery as her hair.

But it was when he'd pushed into her that he'd experienced real pleasure. Even in his subconscious state, he'd responded to the physical pull of his senses. She'd been so hot and wet and deliciously tight, her muscles closing around him, silently urging him on.

And he'd wanted to go on. With her hands cupping his buttocks, her hips lifting to meet his, she'd been desire personified. He thought he'd groaned as she climaxed around him, the reality of his ineptitude intruding at last.

He shuddered now. He'd felt her orgasm, he thought. He'd actually smelled the musky aroma of sex before the images had slipped away. But slip away they had, leaving him to fight his own demons, as weak and defeated as he'd ever felt since he'd come home.

Which was why he'd spent Sunday morning working in the garden. He'd found an ancient lawnmower in the back of the garage and, after siphoning some petrol out of the Land Cruiser, he'd managed to cut the grass at the front of the house. It wasn't very well done, but it had briefly satisfied his need for action. Then he'd gathered a spade and fork and recklessly dug the weeds out of the flower border.

Of course, by lunchtime, his limbs had been trembling with fatigue, and not even a hot bath had eased the pain in his back and thighs. But at least the pain was a physical thing, something he could deal with. Not a pathetic illusion serviced by a phantom.

Diane had rung in the afternoon and he'd had to answer it. He couldn't go on ignoring his calls, but he had made a note to buy an answering machine the next time he went into town.

He'd entertained the brief hope that it might be his mother. But of course it wasn't, and naturally Diane had been peeved that he'd been out the previous day. He hadn't mentioned Fliss. He'd let Diane think he'd been alone, embroidering his story by saying that he hadn't got back until quite late.

'But what were you doing?' Diane asked irritably. 'I thought the whole idea of you moving to the country was that you could get some rest and quiet.'

'What makes you think anything's changed?' he countered, annoyed that she felt she had the right to make judgements. 'I went to the coast, if you must know. I felt like some sea air.'

'Sea air?' Diane snorted. 'You?' She sounded amused. 'Darling, when you want sea air you fly to Cannes or St Tropez. Not some leaky resort on the south coast.'

'That's only your opinion.'

'It used to be yours, too!' Diane exclaimed, her humour vanishing. Then, with an obvious effort, 'Look, why don't we do that next weekend, mmm? Fly to Cannes, I mean. I imagine Hugh's boat's still moored there. He'd be happy to have you

use it. It might persuade him that you weren't serious when
you told him to stuff his job.'

'But I was serious,' said Matt flatly. 'And, for the record, I
didn't tell him to stuff his job.' Hugh Gregory had been his
boss at Thames Valley News and he was still a good friend.
'In any case, I don't have any desire to fly to Cannes. I'm
perfectly happy here.'

'Well, I'm not,' retorted Diane bitterly. 'And if you think I
want to spend my days baking cakes for the local jumble sale
or fielding a stall at the church fête, you're mistaken.'

'In other words, you don't want to be like your mother,'
remarked Matt drily and Diane reacted with predictable vehe-
mence.

'No, I don't,' she snapped peevishly. 'Nor do I want to be
like Fliss Taylor either.' She paused, as if the name had set off
some extra-sensory premonition. 'Have you seen her again, by
the way?'

Matt sighed. He could lie, but what was the point? 'Well, as
she works for me, I'd say that was a no-brainer,' he replied
evenly. 'I'm surprised your mother didn't tell you.'

'You've given her a job!' He'd expected an angry outburst
and he wasn't disappointed. 'My God, Matt, how could you
do such a thing? You know how I feel about that woman.'

Matt only stopped himself from saying that he didn't give a
damn how she felt about it with an effort. Instead, he remained
civil as he said, 'She's a good housekeeper, Diane. Why
shouldn't I employ her? She knows this house better than I
do.'

'Do you think I care if she's good at her job?' Diane was
incensed. 'And to think, I almost drove down to see you yesterday when you didn't answer your phone. I was worried
about you, Matt. But I'd have been mortified if I'd discovered
Fliss Taylor was there.'

He'd have been mortified, too, Matt acknowledged, remembering what he'd been doing the previous afternoon. It would
have been horribly embarrassing if Diane had turned up at the
house. But that was all, he realised with some amazement. He'd

have been embarrassed, but not altogether sorry if she'd found him with Fliss. It would have been easier than having to go on pretending they had a future together.

But he could hardly tell her that over the phone, and, choosing the least provocative option, he said, 'Fliss doesn't work Saturdays.' Which had the virtue of being true.

'Big deal.' Diane was not appeased, her tone turning from resentment to petulance. 'I miss you, Matt. I can't believe you're going to stay there indefinitely.' She sniffed. 'You haven't even said you're sorry I didn't make the trip.'

'Diane—'

'No, I mean it, Matt. I'm beginning to think you don't care about me at all,' she broke in, her voice rising as she spoke. 'If you did, you'd be interested in why I couldn't come. You'd want to know where I was and who I was with.'

Matt blew out a breath. 'OK, tell me,' And then, when she didn't immediately answer him, he added, 'I guess it was something to do with the gallery, yeah?'

Diane hesitated, but as he'd expected she couldn't resist boasting about her achievements. 'Actually, Tony arranged for us to go to Winchester,' she said triumphantly, obviously expecting him to be impressed. 'To see the Charteris Collection. Can you believe that? I mean, the curator almost never allows members of the public to see it, but Tony has a friend who has a friend and he organised it just for me. Wasn't that darling of him?'

Matt suppressed a wry smile. 'Darling,' he agreed mockingly, and he heard her expel an angry breath.

'Of course, I might have known you'd make fun of me,' she snapped, and Matt felt contrite.

'I'm sorry,' he said, not wanting to upset her unnecessarily. 'But forgive me, I don't know what the Charteris Collection is.'

Diane huffed, but she obviously wanted to tell him, and she spent the next few minutes describing the collection of antique snuff boxes in great detail. 'The colours were amazing,' she added. 'Tony and I were absolutely overwhelmed. Of course, he is an expert in fine arts and jewellery, and these little boxes used to be carried by absolutely everyone.'

'Absolutely,' agreed Matt, and then could have bitten out his tongue when Diane pounced on his sardonic response.

'There you go again!' she exclaimed. 'You can't resist it, can you? My work means ab—practically nothing to you. That's why you think I should give it up and move back to Mallon's End.'

'I've never suggested you should give up your job to move back to Mallon's End,' Matt replied wearily. 'I made it clear, right from the start, that this was what I wanted to do. Nothing else.'

'In other words, I don't matter,' Diane snorted. 'You know, I really think you don't care where I go or what I do.' She paused, and then continued defiantly, 'If I told you Tony and I had spent the night together in Winchester, you'd probably still have that smug note in your voice.'

'Sorry,' said Matt, but he didn't sound it. He paused. 'So, did you?'

'Did I what?'

Matt's mouth compressed. He was tempted not to play her game, but perhaps it would be easier for both of them if he did. 'Did you sleep with him?' he repeated, and once again she gave an outraged gasp.

'Of course I didn't sleep with him,' she cried.

'No?'

'No.'

Matt took a gamble. 'Well, it wouldn't be the first time, would it?' he suggested mildly. 'You didn't remain celibate all the time I was away.'

'Matt!' She sounded horrified. 'How can you say such a thing? I was positively devastated when you went missing. Ask your mother. She'll tell you. She was the only person I could turn to, the only one who understood how I was feeling.'

'So Corbett was lying, was he?'

'Tony?' She caught her breath, confused. 'What do you mean?'

Matt chose his words with care. 'He told me he'd comforted you,' he responded casually. 'That you'd turned to him when you needed—emotional relief.'

There was silence for so long that Matt had begun to think she'd hung up on him. But then she burst out chokingly, 'Don't pretend you care!' And Matt knew his gamble had paid off. He'd suspected for some time that Diane's relationship with her boss had changed significantly. He'd just never had the opportunity to test his theory before.

Before he could explain, however, Diane spoke again. 'When did he tell you?' she demanded. A sob thickened her words. 'He swore—he swore he'd never do anything to break us up.'

'He didn't.' Matt heard her sudden intake of breath and continued flatly, 'I may seem brain-dead to you, Diane, but I'm not stupid.'

'You mean—'

'I was only guessing,' he admitted tiredly. 'Corbett said nothing to me.'

'You bastard!'

Diane didn't pretend to mince her words now and Matt decided he deserved that. 'We've both been looking for a way to end this, Diane,' he told her gently. 'It was good while it lasted, but you and I have both moved on.'

'You haven't moved on.' Diane refused to listen to reason. She was hurt and, like a wounded animal, she lashed out. 'If you hadn't tried to be a hero, we wouldn't be having this conversation. I've always known a good story was more important to you than I was.'

'That's not true.'

'Isn't it?' Diane gave a scornful laugh. 'You can't blame me because I have needs only a real man can satisfy.'

Matt stifled a groan. 'I'm not blaming you, Diane—'

'Damn right.' She felt humiliated now and she'd evidently decided she had nothing left to lose. 'Blame yourself. Blame whatever those bastards did to you. But don't blame me for needing something you can't give me anymore.'

'Diane—'

'No, you listen to me. You're not the same man I fell in love with. You've changed, Matt. Really changed. Even your mother has noticed. You're harder, crueller. You don't care about anyone but yourself. Oh, and by the way, you don't need a woman. You've either forgotten—or lost interest in—what to do with one.'

There wasn't much more to say after that, and Matt had put down the phone with a mixture of humiliation and relief.

Which was why he'd taken a bottle of Scotch to bed the night before. Why he had such a God-awful headache this morning. Although Diane's accusation hadn't been even close to the truth, the knowledge that people were judging him for the wrong reasons was mortifying. And, despite how he felt inside, the fact was he didn't have a hope in hell of proving them wrong.

He got up at last, had a long, hot shower and then, feeling marginally better, he dressed in casual khaki trousers and a button-down Oxford shirt. Breakfast was two cups of strong black coffee and two paracetamol tablets. He had no milk or he might have had some cornflakes. The lactose would definitely have put a better lining on his abused stomach.

Whatever, he didn't have a choice and it occurred to him that a trip to the supermarket in Westerbury might be exactly what he needed. Well, perhaps not exactly, but he did need to get out of the house, preferably before Fliss turned up. After the way he'd behaved on Saturday, he wouldn't blame her if she'd decided she didn't want to work for him, after all. But he didn't think he could take any more humiliation right now.

And there was no way he could explain his situation to her without humiliating himself. Even telling her that she inspired feelings in him that no one, not even Diane, had ever done would only sound hypocritical when it was combined with his present inadequacies. She deserved better than that, better than him, even if there was no denying that since meeting her he had found himself entertaining thoughts of how things could be if—

But it was that significant *if* that created the biggest obstacle. Theirs was a tenuous relationship at best and no matter how sympathetic she seemed he doubted it would survive the kind of confession he had to make. She'd accepted his explanation of how he'd got his injuries with real compassion. She hadn't even shown any revulsion when he'd told her about what General Hassan had tried to do. But, she didn't need some pitiful excuse for a man messing up her life—even if he had to fight the almost irresistible temptation to incite her attraction to him.

In the event, Fliss arrived before he could get away. Even though it was only a little after half past eight when he backed the Land Cruiser out of the garage, he returned to the house to collect his keys and wallet and found her waiting in the kitchen.

It was a cooler day, with the threat of rain in the air, and Fliss's hair was a tumbled mass of curls and ringlets. She was wearing jeans and a loose cotton sweater that only hinted at the lush beauty of her breasts. But the denims clung lovingly to every inch of her legs and Matt had to drag his eyes away from them.

She'd evidently walked to work as usual, which would account for the fact that he hadn't heard her approach. He didn't know which of them was the most embarrassed by the sudden encounter, however.

Fliss recovered first. 'Are you going out?' she asked a little stiffly, and Matt realised how bad this must look.

'I was going to ring you,' he said lamely, even though that idea had just occurred to him. He paused. 'You're early.'

'Yes, I know.' Fliss lifted a hand to tuck a silky strand of red-gold hair behind her ear and he badly wanted to touch her. 'I—well, I didn't know if you'd want me to continue working here, and if you didn't I—'

That dispelled his ambivalence and he scowled. 'Why wouldn't I want you to go on working here?' he broke in harshly, even though he'd been having similar thoughts. 'For God's sake, you've done nothing wrong.'

'Diane might not agree with you.'

'F—forget Diane,' Matt amended the instinctive swear-word. He found he was breathing hard in spite of himself. 'Do you want the job or don't you? That's all I need to know.'

Fliss held up her head. 'But you're going out, aren't you? And it's early, as you said. Sometimes you're not even out of bed at this time.'

'Yeah, so?'

She drew her lower lip between her teeth for a moment. 'Are you sure you weren't trying to avoid me?'

Matt sighed. 'All right. Maybe I was.' His lips twisted. 'I'm a coward, so sue me.'

'You're not a coward,' said Fliss fiercely. And then, as if realising she was being too presumptive, she added, 'Anyway, you're just avoiding the issue. Why were you really going out?'

Matt blew out a breath. 'If you must know, I thought you might not want to come back,' he admitted. 'After what happened on Saturday—'

'Forget Saturday,' she said, her soft lips tightening purposefully. 'I have. It was a mistake. On both our parts.' She glanced about her. 'Now, if it's all right with you, I'd like to get on.'

CHAPTER THIRTEEN

'DID I tell you I was talking to Matthew Quinn in the pub the other night?'

George Taylor spoke almost diffidently and Fliss guessed it was because he knew damn well he hadn't said anything about it to her. But then, nor had Matt, she conceded, feeling a ridiculous sense of betrayal. Though why would he? Since the morning a couple of weeks ago when he'd asked her to stay on as his housekeeper, he'd hardly spoken to her.

Now Fliss looked up from the accounts she was doing at the kitchen table and arched an enquiring brow. 'No,' she said, keeping her tone as casual as possible. 'I didn't know you were on friendly terms with him.'

'Well, I wasn't,' said her father drily, pulling out the chair opposite and subsiding into it. 'But Harry Gilchrist was there and he sort of involved me in their conversation.' He paused, waiting for Fliss to say something and when she didn't he went on, 'He seems a decent sort when you get to know him.'

'He is.' Fliss returned to her bookkeeping. 'Does this mean you don't object to my working for him now?'

'Well, I don't like you doing the sort of work you do for anybody,' retorted her father shortly. 'But I suppose, now I've got to know him, I'm not as opposed to it as I was.'

'Good.' Fliss nodded to the books in front of her. 'Because I have to tell you that without me having that job we'd be struggling to make ends meet.'

'All right, all right.' George Taylor didn't like to be reminded of their financial circumstances. 'Anyway, in a couple of years, when Amy goes to the comprehensive in Westerbury, you'll be able to resume your physiotherapy training.'

'Will I?' Fliss wasn't as confident of resuming her training as he was. It was five years since she'd been forced to give it up. Things changed, qualifications changed, and there were bound to be dozens of newly qualified, younger applicants for every vacancy. Changing the subject, she said, 'So—what were you talking to him about?'

'Who? Matthew Quinn?' Fliss gave him a narrow look and he shrugged defensively. 'We were talking about writing, actually,' he said. 'Did you know he's thinking of writing a series of articles for a Sunday newspaper detailing his experiences in Abuqara and giving an insider's view of the reasons for the rebellion? It sounds fascinating stuff.' He paused. 'I've told him that if there's anything I can do—research and so on—he has only to ask.'

'I see.' Fliss's eyes dipped again. 'So you've decided he's not deranged, after all?'

'I never said he was deranged, Felicity.' Her father sounded positively offended now. 'I said there'd been rumours that he'd been traumatised by his months in captivity, that's all. And who wouldn't be? From what he was telling me, it was no picnic.'

'No.' Fliss knew that. The scars on Matt's back were a silent testimony to his suffering, and there was no point in baiting her father with things she didn't really believe.

All the same, she couldn't help feeling a little hurt that Matt should have confided in her father, of all people. It was as if he'd cut her off from any involvement in his life and, after the closeness they'd shared, it was painful. But then, she'd left him in no doubt that she didn't want that kind of relationship with him, so why was she feeling so let down?

All the same, when she arrived at the house the following morning, Fliss was unhappily aware that she was still nursing her grievance. But, dammit, it wasn't her fault that he'd chosen to ruin a perfectly good working relationship by attempting to seduce her, was it?

There was a strange car parked at the side of the house, and although Fliss was in the habit of letting herself into the kitchen, she felt compelled to knock this morning. It could be

Diane, she thought uneasily, and the last thing she wanted was to walk in on a steamy clinch and embarrass them all.

Well, she doubted she'd embarrass Matt, she decided bitterly. He wouldn't care about her feelings any more than he apparently cared about Diane's.

Matt himself opened the door and Fliss, who'd seen little of him in the past two weeks, was instantly struck by his gaunt appearance. She'd tried not to pay attention to him, to get on with the work she was being paid for. But now she was forced to acknowledge that he had that jaded weariness about him again that she'd noticed when she'd first got to know him.

However he still moved with that lithe, predatory grace that never failed to cause such an unwelcome awareness in the pit of her stomach, and when he stepped aside to let her in she ensured that her bare arm didn't brush any part of his lean frame.

His dark eyes narrowed, impaling her with a cool, dangerous gaze, letting her know he had noticed, and she found it difficult to say, 'Good morning,' as she moved into the room.

Matt closed the door and then leaned back on it for a moment, watching her. 'Why didn't you just come in?' he asked, his harsh voice scraping sensuously over her nerves, and she strove for a casual tone.

'I thought you must have company,' she said, setting her backpack on the table. She glanced about her, noting there were two empty coffee mugs on the drainer, and stiffened. 'Is Diane here?'

'No.' Matt's tone was chilly. 'I don't expect to be seeing Diane again.'

'Oh!' Fliss moistened her lips. Did that account for his haggard appearance? 'I'm sorry.'

'Are you?' His thin lips twisted. 'Yeah, well, don't lose any sleep over it. I haven't.'

'You look as if you have,' Fliss exclaimed impulsively, and then wished she hadn't when his expression darkened.

'Thanks.' He was sardonic. 'I can always rely on you to tell it like it is.'

'I didn't mean…' Fliss felt as if she was digging a pit for herself, but she couldn't let him think she didn't care. 'It's just—well, you look tired, that's all.'

'Right.'

'I—perhaps you should get yourself a gardener, after all,' she continued doggedly. She knew he spent most afternoons working in the garden now. 'You've probably overdone it again.'

Matt gave a disbelieving shake of his head. 'How pleasant it must be to live in your world, where every ailment can be explained away in physical terms. I'm looking tired, *ergo* I've been overdoing it. I've got a headache, so I should stop banging my head against this brick wall.'

Fliss felt the colour rise in her cheeks. 'There's no need to be sarcastic,' she said stiffly. 'I realise some things can't be explained away so easily. And whatever you say, I'm sure Diane—'

'For God's sake, will you stop harping on about Diane?' he snapped savagely, and she drew back in surprise.

This was a side of him she'd never seen before and, as if realising he'd alarmed her, Matt came away from the door. Putting a hand on the table at either side of her, he imprisoned her within his arms. 'Don't look at me like that,' he implored her roughly. 'I'd never hurt you, surely you know that?' His eyes dropped to her mouth and she quivered in spite of herself. 'And don't ever think Diane has any bearing on the way I'm feeling now, because she doesn't.'

'And I can vouch for that,' remarked a dry voice behind them, and Fliss, who had been wondering if Matt was going to kiss her again and speculating about what she would do if he did, started violently.

Matt reacted considerably less urgently, pushing himself away from the table—and Fliss—with weary resignation. Then, as Fliss glanced somewhat apprehensively over her shoulder to see a much older woman watching them, he said flatly, 'This is my mother, Fliss. I don't believe you've met.'

'As if that was in question,' observed Mrs Quinn crisply,

coming further into the room. She was a tall, elderly woman, with iron-grey hair, dressed in an elegant silk suit. 'How do you do—Felicity, is it? I understand you've worked wonders in this house.'

Fliss licked her dry lips. 'Um—Fliss will do,' she murmured, glancing awkwardly at Matt's set face. 'And I—er—I've just done my job, that's all.'

'Rather more than that, from what I hear,' declared the other woman smoothly. She, too, glanced at her son. 'Isn't that right, Matt?'

'If you say so.' He was remote.

'I do say so.' His mother seemed unmoved by his obvious withdrawal. 'You two evidently know one another very well.' She paused. 'Is there something I should know?'

'No!'

Matt's denial was violent, and Fliss felt something inside her curl up and die. Whatever might have happened if his mother hadn't interrupted them clearly meant nothing to him.

'That's not what Diane says,' Mrs Quinn murmured softly, and once again her son lost his cool.

'I don't give a—a damn what Diane says,' he snarled, and Fliss knew he was moderating his language for his mother's benefit. 'What do I have to do to make you both understand that I couldn't care less about Diane?'

'Now that I can believe,' remarked his mother mildly. 'But you used to. And the poor girl can't understand what she's done for you to treat her so shabbily. Especially if you're living here alone.'

'Can't she?'

Matt's tone was mocking now, but Mrs Quinn was not prepared to back down. 'No,' she replied pleasantly. 'She seems to think there's something going on between you and...' Her eyes flickered briefly in Fliss's direction. 'Well, between you and this young lady, actually.' Her dark brows arched in enquiry. 'Is she wrong?'

'Yes.'

Matt's response was immediate, and Fliss wished the floor

would just open up and swallow her. He'd had no hesitation in dismissing his relationship with her. Whatever was going on between them, it was not something he was prepared to own up to.

She shifted awkwardly, desperately wishing she was not a part of this conversation. But when Matt looked at her, instead of at his mother, what she saw in his gaze confused her even more.

Hot and passionate, his eyes ate her up. It was an almost palpable invasion that turned her legs to water. Banked fires burned behind his gaze, yet she had the sense he was still determined not to give in to them. But he wanted her; she could see it. What power was controlling him that was so much darker than his natural will?

She was mesmerised for several mindless seconds, and then his mother spoke again, destroying the tenuous bond between them. 'Well,' she said, 'if there is no one else, I don't understand your attitude. When you were captured, when you were a prisoner in Abuqara—'

'Diane was screwing her boss's brains out,' Matt finished for her harshly. He started towards the door as if he'd had enough of her interrogation. 'Ask her about it. See if she denies it. But you know what? She did us both a favour.' His lips parted in a grim smile. 'I'm no good for any woman, and that includes Fliss.'

He strode out of the room then, without looking at either of them again, and Fliss turned abruptly towards the sink. She felt sick, and empty, and she snatched up the two dirty coffee mugs and started washing up. But her eyes were burning, and she had to blink several times to clear them.

The room was silent behind her and, guessing Mrs Quinn had followed her son, she glanced over her shoulder. But to her surprise, and dismay, she found the woman still standing where she'd been before, dark eyes, so unnervingly like Matt's, regarding Fliss with an intent appraisal.

'Oh!'

Fliss couldn't prevent the shocked exclamation and Mrs

Quinn held up an apologetic hand. 'I'm sorry. Did I startle you?'

Twice, thought Fliss tensely, swinging round again before Matt's mother could see her tear-wet eyes. But she should have known better than to think she could fool a close relative of his.

'You're upset,' Mrs Quinn said gently. 'I'm afraid my son has that effect on people. Or rather he has since he got back from North Africa.'

'I've got something in my eye, that's all,' said Fliss, not prepared to confide in her. Then, when the woman still didn't go away, 'Can I get you something? Have you had breakfast?'

'You don't have to pretend with me,' insisted the older woman sympathetically. 'Matt can be utterly charming when he puts his mind to it. And, obviously, he's taken quite a fancy to you. But you must understand, there's no future in it.'

'Do you think I don't know that?' Much as she wanted to remain silent, Fliss didn't like being patronised in this way. 'As your son said, there's nothing between him and me.'

'But you'd like there to be?'

Fliss pressed her lips together. 'I must get on,' she said, refusing to satisfy the woman's mordant curiosity. Then, with a coolness she was quite proud of, 'Will you be staying for a few days? If so, I'll make sure there are plenty of towels in your bathroom.'

Matt's mother stayed for four days and during that time Fliss made sure that she and the other woman were never alone again. It wasn't difficult, the weekend making up two of the days. She knew that what Mrs Quinn had told her was true, but that didn't mean she had to listen to her. Besides, despite what Matt had said about Diane having an affair with her boss, Fliss suspected his mother still hoped he would forgive her. And why not? Diane was blonde and beautiful, and successful. Exactly the sort of wife a man like him should have.

Deciding whether or not she should stay on at the Old Coaching House as Matt's housekeeper was another matter, however. Mrs Quinn's visit had made certain things clear to her, and one of them was the total futility of her attraction to her employer.

So, the question was, could she go on working here knowing that any feelings she had for him were not reciprocated? Oh, she suspected he would not be averse to having an affair with her, but did she really want to risk the pain that an abortive relationship with him would bring? The decision was far harder to make than it should have been.

In consequence, she was still in a state of uneasy confusion when she arrived at the house the morning after Matt's mother had returned to London. Mrs Quinn had been packing when Fliss left the previous day, and although she'd suspected the older woman would have liked to have another warning word with her, Fliss had deliberately left stripping the bed in the spare room until today. She'd wanted no more advice, no more homilies on the uselessness of falling in love with Matt. Indeed, it would give her a great deal of pleasure to clean the room Mrs Quinn had used, knowing as she did so that her enemy had departed.

No, not her enemy, she corrected herself impatiently as she opened the door that led into the kitchen. Matt's mother meant well. She just couldn't see how a common housekeeper, a single mother, moreover, could have anything to offer her son.

There was no sign of Matt this morning, but that wasn't unusual. He generally unlocked the back door for her and then either went to take his shower or, if he was already dressed, he might work in the library all morning. Since her father had told her about the series of articles he was planning to write, she'd assumed he was working on them, although his schedule had obviously been interrupted while his mother was here.

Occasionally he was still in bed when she arrived, but those occasions were rare and usually coincided with the after-effects of work he'd done in the garden. Despite her offer to help him find a gardener, he'd insisted on doing everything himself, and she could only speculate that he expunged his lingering frustrations in physical effort.

Though not frustrations about her, she assured herself grimly. Whatever he felt for her, it was obviously easily mastered and since the scene with his mother he'd given her no reason to believe that he regretted anything he'd said.

Which should have made her decision as to whether to keep this job easier, but somehow it didn't. She was a fool, she thought irritably. She was letting him treat her any way he chose and she was too weak—or too stupid—to do anything about it.

Surprisingly, there was no dirty coffee mug on the drainer this morning. No sign that he'd had any breakfast either, and she decided he must still be in bed. Not that it mattered to her, she determined firmly. She had plenty to occupy her. Not least, his mother's bed to strip, the sheets to put in the washer, and the adjoining bathroom to clean. That would take her over an hour and by then he would probably be up.

But he wasn't.

Even though she'd stripped and remade the spare bed, removed all the odds and ends of cotton wool and used tissues from the vanity in the bathroom, scoured the bath and basin, and finally vacuumed the carpet, there was no movement from Matt's room.

Which was unusual—and worrying, she conceded, not knowing if she ought to check to see if he was all right. She had thought she'd heard something from time to time, but, remembering the other occasion when she'd gone to his bedroom, she was chary about appearing too forward. She knew him better now, of course—some might say too well, she acknowledged unhappily. Yet well enough to feel some responsibility if there was a chance he might be ill.

To give herself time to decide what she ought to do—or maybe to give him more time to wake up—she decided to go downstairs again and make herself a cup of coffee. The caffeine would be welcome and it would be ready if he needed it, too.

She was at the top of the stairs when she heard an unusual noise. She thought it sounded as if someone was in pain, and as Matt was the only other person in the house, it had to be him.

But what was he doing? It was a strange sound, as if—as if he was moaning, she decided uneasily. Or snoring, she amended, trying to be positive. He could be sound asleep and she was imagining the worst.

She hesitated. As usual, his bedroom door was ajar. She'd determined he kept it that way because of his months in captivity. She'd guessed he liked the idea that the door was open, that he could walk out of the room whenever he chose. But he wasn't walking out now, and despite her misgivings she had to find out why.

The sound was louder when she opened the door, and she couldn't help feeling as if she had no right to be there. But someone had to help him, and as she stepped towards the bed a shiver of apprehension slithered down her spine.

He wasn't snoring, she saw at once. If anything, he was groaning, and the way he was threshing about on his pillows made her sure he was in pain. Yet his eyes were closed, and even when she said his name they didn't open. Instead, behind his lids his pupils were moving agitatedly, causing a flickering motion that was a little scary in itself.

'Matt,' she said tentatively. And then when that elicited no response, 'Are you all right?'

He was nude beneath the thin sheet, and she was half-afraid he'd throw off even that covering. 'Matt,' she said again, wishing he would wake up. But he didn't. He seemed deeply unconscious and she guessed it was the dream he was having that was causing him so much grief.

She didn't need to think very hard to know what he was dreaming about, however. After the experiences he had had, who could wonder? This probably happened all the time, only she wasn't usually around to witness it. He'd told her he often had trouble sleeping and she wasn't surprised if all his dreams were as frightening as the one he was having at present.

Then he spoke, and for a moment she thought her wish had been granted. But his eyes were still closed and the words that spilled disjointedly from his lips were not the kind of thing he would ever say to her. A stream of curses and profanities, some in English, some in a language she suspected might be Arabic, but all equally offensive, or so it seemed, filled the room.

Fliss didn't know what to do. She wanted to wake him up. That seemed the most sensible course of action. But how would he feel when he discovered she had been a witness to his distress?

Yet did that matter, when she was already considering handing in her notice? It didn't really figure what he thought of her so long as he was all right.

Swallowing, she put out a hand to touch the arm nearest to her, but before she could do so he reared up off his pillows. 'Don't touch me, you filthy bastard!' he snarled, and she saw to her dismay that his eyes were open now. He was looking straight at her, his stare dark and glassy and filled with hate, and she gazed back, aghast. He was speaking to her, she realised sickly. Oh, God, did he really despise her that much?

CHAPTER FOURTEEN

HORROR gripped her. This was so much worse than she'd anticipated. What did he think she'd been about to do to him? Take advantage of him? Seduce him? She had never felt so devastated in her life.

'I—Matt—'

It was all she could do to say his name, but it seemed to have an instant effect. Amazingly, his eyes changed. The glassy, hate-filled stare disappeared, replaced by a look of almost horrified comprehension. 'Fliss,' he croaked weakly. 'Oh, hell, Fliss, what are you doing here?'

Fliss could hardly get her explanation out. 'I—I was worried about you,' she stammered, praying he would believe her. 'You—you were making a weird noise. I—I thought you must be having a bad dream.'

'Oh, was I ever.' Matt collapsed back against his pillows again, and, although he closed his eyes for a moment, she knew there was no danger of him falling back to sleep. 'God, I'm sorry.' He opened his eyes again and now there was no trace of the stranger who had sworn at her. 'I frightened you, didn't I? I can see I did.' He held out his hand towards her. 'Forgive me.'

Fliss's legs were trembling so much, she was amazed they continued to support her, and she was more than willing to let him take her hand and draw her to the bed. 'Sit,' he said huskily, pulling her down beside him. 'You look as if you've seen a ghost.'

'Not a ghost. A monster, maybe,' she admitted weakly, and he expelled a rueful breath.

'I'm sorry,' he said again. He paused, and then went on

bleakly, 'It's some time since I've had that particular dream. I guess I'm not going to escape it quite yet.'

Fliss nodded. 'You—what you said—you weren't speaking to me, were you?'

'As I don't remember saying anything, I doubt it.' His brows drew together and she wondered if he was aware his thumb was making circles on her palm. She didn't think so, but when he lifted her hand to his lips, she couldn't be sure of anything anymore. His tongue brushed over her knuckles. 'What did I say?' And when she didn't answer, he turned her hand and bestowed a moist kiss to her palm. 'Tell me.'

She shook her head. 'I'd rather not.'

'That bad, was it?'

'Pretty bad,' she agreed, quivering a little as he continued to play with her fingers. 'I guess you don't want to talk about it?'

'No.'

Matt was very definite about that and she was suddenly aware of the intimacy of the situation. She couldn't forget he was naked beneath the sheet and the warm pressure of his thigh against her hip was a tantalising reminder.

He looked at her then, and she dipped her head in embarrassment. She suspected what she was thinking was there in her face for all to see and this was definitely not the time to be having such thoughts.

But averting her eyes had its dangers, too. The sheet didn't quite cover his navel and she was treated to a disturbing glimpse of the arrowing dark hair that grew thicker around his manhood. The sheet stirred, and her heart almost stopped beating. He was becoming aroused, she thought uneasily, and they were alone in the house. Did she really want this to happen?

She ought to leave, she told herself. She should get out of there before something irrevocable occurred. She didn't want to, she admitted. What she really wanted to do was crawl into bed with him. To hold him in her arms and comfort him. But that wasn't going to happen and with her history it was obviously the last thing she should do.

But he was still holding her hand and she didn't want to

make a complete fool of herself by getting into a tugging match with him. 'Well, if you're all right,' she murmured, hoping he would get the message and let her go. But he didn't.

'Hey,' he said instead, and she was obliged to meet his probing gaze. 'What's wrong? I'm not embarrassing you, am I?'

'Embarrassing me?' Fliss managed to sound as if what he'd said was totally off the wall. 'No, of course you're not embarrassing me.' She wet her dry lips with the tip of her tongue and looked pointedly at his brown fingers caressing her pale flesh. 'Um—can I have my hand back, please?'

Matt's lips twisted. 'What if I don't want to let you go?'

Fliss's laugh was nervous. 'Then I'd have to use force,' she said, struggling to keep her tone light. 'Come on, Matt. I've got to get on.'

She felt his eyes on her face then and, although she didn't want to meet his gaze, she couldn't seem to stop herself. He might be disturbing, he might be dangerous, but she wouldn't have been human if she wasn't excited by his unpredictability.

'You don't have to be afraid of me, you know,' he murmured, lifting his other hand and trailing it deliberately down her cheek. 'I might want to touch you, but I can't hurt you.'

Don't you believe it, thought Fliss, remembering the last time he'd touched her in intimate detail. Already her heart was beating faster than it should and a trickle of perspiration was making its way between her breasts. Any minute now, she was going to say or do something equally stupid and she couldn't have that.

'I'd still like my hand back,' she said, unable to think of a more original response. And then, because she had to make him understand, 'We—we both know this isn't going anywhere, Matt. So why spoil a good working relationship with—well, with sex?' She forced a smile. 'Just let me go.'

Matt laughed then. But it wasn't a nervous laugh as hers had been. Nor was it a particularly humorous one either, and she wondered what she'd said to provoke it. There was a bleak expression in his eyes, too, that spoke of memories best forgotten, and she felt a latent sense of contrition for inadvertently reminding him of the past again.

'Matt,' she murmured pleadingly, wanting to placate him and comfort him and not really knowing how. 'I didn't mean that the way it sounded.'

'Didn't you?' She doubted he believed her. 'Well, it was a reasonable enough supposition. We're alone here, and you have every right to assume that I might want to take advantage of you.'

'I wouldn't assume that.' Fliss wanted to groan at her own inadequacy. 'Look…' She paused. 'If I'm afraid, it's of what I might do if—if you did try to seduce me.'

Matt's mouth took on a mocking curve. '*Try* being the operative word,' he said, in a strange dry voice. 'Oh, Fliss!' This time when he spoke his voice was thick with emotion. 'You are such a contradiction.' And putting a hand behind her head, he pulled her down to him.

Fliss tried to remember that just moments before she'd been determined this wouldn't happen, but she was lost from the start. When he kissed her, his mouth hot and demanding on hers, his tongue forcing its way into her mouth, she could do nothing less than respond. His hand at her nape slanted her mouth across his, deepened and hardened the kiss until she was breathless and gasping for air.

She tried to keep her feet on the ground, both metaphorically and physically, but when he rolled over on the bed, imprisoning her beneath him, the possibilities of either went out the window. Somehow the sheet had been sacrificed in the hungry tangle of their bodies and all she could feel was the warm, muscular weight of his body pinning her to the bed.

And it was such a delicious feeling. One muscled thigh was lying between her legs, which meant that her skirt must be caught up somewhere around her hips, but she couldn't seem to care. Even the knowledge that her plain cotton underwear must be vastly different from what he was used to didn't arouse more than a fleeting regret. This was where she wanted to be, and if that meant she was wicked she would deal with it later.

Right now, it was enough that Matt was kissing her with an urgency that matched her own, and she was wasted.

'You know this is crazy, don't you?' he breathed a little unsteadily into the hollow of her neck, but Fliss didn't want to listen. Instead, she gripped his head and brought his mouth back to hers. Recriminations could come later, she thought fiercely, when this feverish madness was a thing of the past, too.

And despite what he'd said, Matt couldn't seem to control what was happening either. His overnight stubble was a welcome abrasion when he trailed searing kisses down her throat, and she felt the calluses that gardening had made on his hands when he pushed his fingers beneath the cropped hem of her T-shirt.

His hands stroked her midriff, as they'd done before, but then they moved upward to cup the swelling mounds of her breasts. Within her bra, her nipples felt rock-hard and painfully engorged, and she shifted restlessly when all he did was press his palms against them through the bra.

'Fliss…' he groaned, but she couldn't let him voice his doubts now. Scrabbling behind her back, she managed to release the clasp of the bra, and allowed a little moan to escape her when his hard fingers touched her sensitive flesh.

'God, Fliss,' he muttered now, but this time there was no reluctance in his words. She moaned again when he pushed her T-shirt up above her breasts and took one swollen peak into his mouth.

His tongue circled her nipple almost greedily before sucking strongly on the tip. Then he moved purposefully to her other breast, and she felt a pleasurable pain envelop her. The rush of heat it engendered flooded down into her belly, and she trembled with emotions she knew she'd never experienced before.

A pulse was beating between her legs, a throbbing ache that she sensed only he could satisfy. In a fleeting moment of coherence she wondered if this was what romance authors meant when they said the heroine was consumed by her own body's desires. That was how she felt: consumed, and reckless, and blind to the dangers he now—and always had—represented.

He pushed her T-shirt over her head and Fliss felt her hair come loose from the pony-tail in which she'd confined it that morning. He said something unintelligible as he dropped her bra over the side of the bed and buried his face in her hair. Then she heard him whisper hoarsely, 'You smell incredible.'

So do you, she acknowledged silently, the clean male scent of his skin made all the more sensual by his body's heat. There was the faintest trace of musk, too, and this potent evidence of his maleness made her feel weak and dizzy with need.

That was when she identified the growing pressure beside her hip. It was so long since she'd been with a man that she hadn't realised until now what was happening. But then, the abortive little affair she'd had with Terry Matheson was not something to remember. And he had felt nothing like this: so big and powerful, his erection pulsing against her leg.

Her skirt was up around her waist now and she thought Matt's hand shook a little as he cupped her through her panties. 'You're wet,' he said thickly, and she realised he could feel her arousal clear through the thin cotton.

'I know,' she said, half apologetically, and she heard the groan that rumbled through his chest at her words.

'Hell, Fliss,' he muttered, pulling her panties down to her knees and spreading the cluster of red-gold curls with his thumb, 'that is so not something to be ashamed of.' And before she knew what he intended, he slid down her body until his mouth was level with the tight curls at the tops of her legs.

She couldn't believe what he was doing, but although her hands moved futilely to clutch his hair, his thrusting tongue defeated her. Sensations such as she'd never experienced before gathered into a burning coil she couldn't control and, in spite of wanting to wait until he was a part of her before she came, her orgasm was irresistible. And overwhelming. An incredible wave of pleasure swept her up and over the brink, the shuddering aftermath drenching him with the sweetness of her essence. Then, as she struggled back to sanity, he slid over her again and let her taste herself on his lips.

It was all totally unreal, totally erotic, and Fliss felt as if her whole body was engulfed in fire. But that breathtaking orgasm had left her only partially satisfied. She wanted more; she wanted *him;* and she was horrified when Matt abruptly rolled away from her.

She gasped in disbelief. There was no way she was going to let him pleasure her without pleasuring himself, she thought passionately, and she had no hesitation about tearing off her skirt and kicking her panties the rest of the way down her legs. Then she was as naked as he was, and positioning herself so that she was looking down at him, she bent and covered his mouth with her own.

'Fliss…'

He spoke her name against her lips, his eyes wide now and filled with a haunting regret she refused to accept. He wanted her; she knew he did. And, despite his apparent denial, she found that when she circled his mouth with her tongue his lips parted almost automatically.

He liked it, she assured herself, not understanding his resistance but eager to build on her success. With instinctive daring, she dipped her tongue into his mouth, letting it slide the length of his in a tentative exploration.

A feeling not unlike exultation gripped her when she felt his response. His quickening breathing filled her nose and mouth, filled her lungs, and she felt as if she was drowning in the scent and feel of him. Dipping her head even lower, she bit one of his button-hard nipples, and the sound he made then was definitely not a protest.

However, when she began to drop a chain of moist kisses down his chest to his flat stomach, and her fingers moved unmistakably towards his groin, his reaction was much different. His hand shot out and trapped her fingers in an iron-hard grasp and in a muffled undertone he grated, 'No!'

Fliss's immediate thought was to obey him. After all, hers was a fragile confidence at best, and she wasn't used to going against authority. But then, the expression in his eyes made her hesitate, and, although she didn't fight to continue, she didn't draw back either. Something was going on here, something she didn't yet understand. But she intended to, she told herself grimly. Oh, yes, she intended to.

'You want me,' she said, her voice almost as low as his had been, and she saw him close his eyes as if he couldn't bear to let her see the truth in them. 'You do,' she insisted huskily. And then, because it was the only thing she could think of to explain his behaviour, she added, 'I'm not asking you to make any commitment. I realise that Diane—'

'It's not Diane,' he snarled, and once again she was assailed with the fear that perhaps she was wrong. Perhaps he didn't want her, after all. But then, in a hoarse voice, he continued, 'Of course I want you, dammit. I'd give anything if I could—' He broke off, staring at her with tortured eyes. 'But I can't. Do you understand? I can't. I'm impotent, Fliss. That's what those bastards did to me. I only have to think about sex—' He groaned. 'That's why I can't make love to you as I want to. I'm no good to you. I'm no good to any woman.'

The silence that followed his outburst was significant only for its brevity. But then Fliss exclaimed incredulously, 'I don't believe it!'

'Believe it.' Matt spoke heavily. 'Do you think I'd make something like that up?'

'But—you were aroused—'

'Only slightly.'

'No.' Fliss wouldn't have that. 'I felt it, beside my hip. You were hard. I felt you throbbing against my leg.'

'You imagined it.'

Matt responded harshly, but Fliss knew what she'd felt; what she'd seen, for God's sake, before he'd decided that only one of them was going to be satisfied.

'I know what I felt, Matt,' she cried, but he closed his eyes again as if this was all too much for him to bear.

'Just—just leave me, huh?' he said tiredly, and now when she glanced towards his groin she saw he had some reason for his despair. He was soft and flaccid again, the power of his erection destroyed by his own disbelief.

She sat back on her heels then, not sure what she ought to do. If he was right and she stayed here, she was only exacerbating his misery. But if she was right—and she was almost sure she was—this might be her only chance to prove it to him.

Deciding she had nothing to lose, she leant forward and laid her hand against his cheek. And, as she'd anticipated, Matt reacted violently. Thrusting her hand aside, he attempted to roll away from her, but she was too quick for him. Moving more positively than she would have ever thought possible, she straddled him, sitting across his hips and pinning him to the bed.

'What the hell—?' he began, but she refused to let him ruin this by losing his temper.

Putting a finger across his lips, she leant towards him until her breasts brushed his chest. Then, cupping them in her hands, she presented them to him with a smile that was unashamedly seductive.

'Are you mad?' he exclaimed, but she saw him looking at her, saw the way his eyes darkened with unwilling awareness as she shifted against his hip; when he realised her moistness was brushing his groin.

'What you did to me,' she said huskily. 'Will you do it again?' She looked down at herself deliberately. 'I sort of— ache, if you know what I mean.'

'God, Fliss—'

'Or I could do it for you,' she murmured daringly, and knew an incredible sense of triumph when she felt him hardening beneath her.

'You don't know what you're talking about,' he choked harshly, but she knew exactly what she was doing. She might have little experience when it came to men, but she'd read enough books to know that actions definitely spoke louder than words.

'We'll see, shall we?' she said, not knowing where all this confidence was coming from. She leant closer so that her breasts were crushed against his chest now and traced his lips with her tongue. 'Hmm, you taste good.'

'Fliss…'

There was a note of desperation in his voice, but it didn't seem to be having any effect on his body's reactions, thank goodness. When Fliss shuffled backward, his erection rose almost proudly from its coarse nest of hair, and she encircled it with her hand before bending to take him into her mouth.

He jerked convulsively then, but she didn't give up. Her tongue loved the silken length of him, and she got a particular pleasure from feeling his heartbeat pulsing against the roof of her mouth. His skin was like velvet, and she tried to imagine how good it would feel to have that soft-coated hardness inside her.

'Please…' he groaned, and she knew that, however convinced she was that Matt wasn't impotent as he believed, there was only one way to prove it. Not without some trepidation, she rose onto her knees and positioned herself above him. Then, before he could stop her, before she lost the courage to do it, she lowered herself onto him.

Her first thought was that she'd been too ambitious. She couldn't do this. He was too big, and she was too tight, and it seemed as if she simply wouldn't be capable of accommodating him. But, despite Matt's hoarse cry of protest, she persisted, and found to her relief that her body expanded to meet his needs. Seconds later, he was nestled slickly inside her, stretching her and filling her in a way she could never have imagined before this moment.

She looked at Matt, half hoping to see approval in his eyes, but he had half reared up on his pillows, and there was pain, but no approbation, in his expression.

'Fliss,' he muttered, his hands reaching for her hips, and she guessed he was going to lift her off him.

'Matt,' she countered, leaning forward to silence him with a kiss, and he slumped back again almost helplessly.

But despite his resistance, the kiss was like no other they had exchanged. It was hot, and passionate, and soul-deep, and almost destructive in its intensity. It was an open-mouthed affirmation of how good they were together, and, almost without her being aware of what she was doing, Fliss began to move.

With her hands pressed on the pillows at either side of his head, her first foray was almost tentative. But it was so good, made her feel so good, that she repeated the exercise. And, although she was sure Matt still believed she was wasting her time, he couldn't prevent his own automatic participation.

Their kisses grew hotter, wetter, more and more uncontrolled, and pretty soon Fliss was rearing back to ride him like the stallion he really was. And as if Matt at last believed that there might—there just might—be something in what she'd asserted, he rolled her over again and took over the dominant position.

Fliss didn't know how many times she climaxed during that wild possession. At least three times that she knew of before Matt himself gained his release. And gain his release he did, trembling and sweating though he was. But superbly replete at last, shouting his triumph to the world in general and to Fliss in particular…

CHAPTER FIFTEEN

'CAN I come to Matt's house with you this morning?' asked Amy excitedly, and Fliss, who had been wondering whether she ought to turn up as usual herself, regarded her daughter with doubtful eyes.

'I don't know, poppet,' she said, aware that her father was listening with interest to their conversation. 'Grandad's going to be here all morning. Why not ask Kelly over to play?'

'I don't want to play with Kelly,' said Amy at once, and Fliss thought that was par for the course. '''Sides, her mother's prob'ly taking her shopping. That's what she always does, when we have a lavatory day off school.'

'A what?'

Fliss was immediately diverted from her own problems, and Amy gave her a mischievous look. 'Well, Mrs Hill said it was a loo day,' she pointed out innocently. 'And that's what you always say when you're going to the bathroom.'

'A lieu day!' exclaimed Fliss, as her father chuckled behind his paper. She spelled it out. 'And don't pretend you didn't know.'

Amy grinned. 'Well, it made you smile,' she said, tilting her head to one side appealingly. 'Can I come? Please. I'm sure Matt won't mind.'

'Mr Quinn,' Fliss corrected her shortly, and then, conscious that her father might pick something up from her expression that she didn't want him to see, she said, 'I'm going to make the beds. I'll think about it, OK?'

'OK.'

Amy had to be content with that, but as Fliss left the room she was aware that her father's eyes followed her and she guessed he was curious about her attitude, too.

And who could blame him? Since she'd got back from the Old Coaching House the day before, she had been unusually subdued, and she doubted her father had accepted her assertion that she was tired. Sooner or later, he was going to demand an explanation and, quite honestly, she didn't have one for him.

The truth was, she didn't know how she felt. Oh, she had no doubts about her feelings for Matt, but that wasn't really the problem. Matt was; and, despite what he'd told her the day before, she was having a hard time believing it had been anything more than a spur-of-the-moment thing, brought on by gratitude and nothing else. He didn't really care about her. Goodness, until yesterday morning he'd believed he was impotent. Not exactly the condition in which to swear undying love for anyone. Even Diane.

Especially Diane.

And that was the crux of the matter. Everything Matt had said and done since he arrived at the Old Coaching House had been based on that spurious principle. However kind he had been to her or to Amy, he'd believed there had never been any question of their relationship progressing beyond a certain point. He liked her, he liked Amy; but anything else had just been wishful thinking on her part.

Even remembering the two occasions before yesterday when he'd kissed her took on a different aspect now. With hindsight, she suspected they had just been abortive attempts to prove his own lack of sexuality, and he'd always drawn back before she could discover what was going on.

It hurt to think he might have been using her in that way, but she had no real proof of that either. And despite what had happened the day before, she might be beating herself up over nothing.

Nevertheless, as she shook pillows and smoothed sheets, she couldn't help marvelling at the way she had behaved. She, Fliss Taylor, single mother and full-time housewife, whose only claim to success was three years at university and a one-year stint as a trainee physiotherapist, with one failed relationship behind her, had seduced Matt Quinn, TV journalist, erstwhile prisoner of war, and known celebrity.

It was incredible. Even now, she had difficulty remembering how she had had the nerve to behave as she had. She wasn't—she had never been—the kind of woman to believe she was attractive to men. Well, not to men like him, anyway. Her usual dates were with people like herself: working men, who considered a meal at the pub or a trip to the cineplex in Westerbury constituted an exciting evening out.

Matt wasn't like that. Until he'd been captured and imprisoned in Abuqara, he'd attended society parties and film premières, he'd regarded mixing with socialites and politicians as all in a day's work. He'd travelled the world. He'd spoken about visiting Australia as if it were just across the English Channel, whereas she'd be hard-pressed to afford a package tour to Majorca. The gulf between them was immense and just because yesterday morning the lines had become blurred didn't mean they didn't still exist.

Yet, at the time, it had seemed the only thing she could do. She'd been so high on sex and adrenalin, she hadn't thought twice about acting in a way that was totally alien to her normal nature. She'd acted like a—like a *femme fatale,* for God's sake, and, amazingly, it had worked.

Whatever misgivings she had, and she had to admit that these misgivings were probably all on her own part, she had succeeded. Somehow, and even now she hardly understood how she'd done it, she'd proved to Matt that he was not the useless weakling he'd thought he was. The sex they'd shared had been wild and passionate and incredibly moving, and at the end he'd been totally sated, totally grateful.

But it was his gratitude that she'd found so hard to take. She hadn't wanted that, hadn't wanted to feel that all her efforts had aroused in him was an obligation to thank her in whatever way he believed she wanted. She hadn't expected him to say he *loved* her, for heaven's sake. She hadn't wanted that. Not when she knew that until that moment of revelation in his bedroom all he'd felt for her was a simple affection.

An affection that was primarily based on the way he'd treated her that morning, she acknowledged ruefully. For reasons best known to himself, he'd decided to give her a taste of what she was missing. Why had he done it? To reassure her after the shock he'd given her earlier? Or because he'd felt sorry for her all along, a single woman alone, with very little going on in her life to get excited about?

Whatever, the end result had been the same. She had learned again that it really was dangerous to play with fire, and he had recovered not just his virility, but his belief in himself, too.

She sighed now, lifting the veritable army of soft toys Amy had on her bed onto their usual place on the window-sill. If only she'd left while Matt was in the shower, she thought wearily. Then he wouldn't have said what he did and she wouldn't be feeling such a fool now. They might even have been able to forget the whole incident. Unlikely perhaps, but not impossible. After all, she had made it pathetically clear that she'd expected no commitment from him.

It hadn't happened that way, however. Like the idiot she was, when Matt had said he was going to take a shower, she'd hurriedly put her clothes on and gone downstairs. It hadn't occurred to her that it might be easier all round if she just gave herself the rest of the day off, that if he wanted to speak to her, he knew where she lived. If she had, the ball would have been in his court, so to speak, and she wouldn't be suffering all this soul-searching now.

Instead, she'd been so bemused by what had happened that she hadn't looked beyond the end of her nose. By the time Matt came downstairs, barefoot as usual, and smelling deliciously of soap and shampoo, and clean male flesh, she'd made fresh coffee and was standing at the open back door, a mug of the aromatic beverage in her hand.

She supposed, if she was honest with herself, she'd been too embarrassed to face him, and he'd come up behind her and wrapped his arms about her waist. Then, as she was struggling not to spill her coffee, he'd buried his face in the warm angle of her neck and shoulder. 'I love you, Fliss Taylor, do you know that?' he'd murmured huskily, and for a moment her heart had leapt into her throat. But then he'd spoiled everything by continuing, 'My God, you don't know what you've done for me. I'll never be able to thank you.'

That was when she'd eased herself out of his arms and done what she should have done half an hour before. 'You don't have to thank me,' she had said stiffly, moving to the sink and tipping the remains of her coffee down the drain. And then, 'I—would you mind if I went home and took a shower? I—feel—well, dirty.'

It wasn't the kindest choice of words, she'd known that instantly. Still, she hadn't been too worried about sparing his feelings after the way he'd behaved. She couldn't believe he'd actually said he loved her. For heaven's sake, what did he think? That she'd be flattered? That she'd believe him? Her breath caught in her throat. He didn't love her any more than she liked the image of herself as his mistress.

After what had happened when she was a teenager, she'd always sworn she would never get herself into a situation like this again. She loved her daughter dearly, and she wouldn't be without her, but she wanted no more unplanned pregnancies. One mistake, taking into account her age, could be forgiven. But she was too old now not to appreciate the dangers of unprotected sex, however justified the cause. Too old to withstand the stigma of knowing the whole village was gossiping about her, as they would if it happened again.

She'd known Matt had been taken aback by her response, but she couldn't help it. She might have behaved recklessly by having sex with him, but she wanted him to understand that she didn't need his guilty confession.

Consequently, when he'd said, 'If that's what you want,' she'd ignored his obvious confusion and taken him at his word. Whether he'd expected her to go back later she had no way of knowing, but she'd decided that giving them both twenty-four hours breathing space was probably the wisest course.

The trouble was, the twenty-four hours were over now—or almost—and she was still no surer of what she wanted to do.

Could she go on working for him after what had happened? Would he want her to? And how would she cope with the emotional fallout if he decided it would be simpler for all concerned if they just called it a day?

Downstairs again, Amy was waiting expectantly for her decision and Fliss acknowledged that it might be easier all round if she took the child with her. It would mean that she and Matt would have no chance for any private conversation, and that was all to the good. For her, at least. It would give her another twenty-four hours' grace, and she found she needed that.

'Tell Matt I found a website that deals almost exclusively with military dictatorships,' said her father as Fliss was preparing to leave. 'I'm sure he'll be interested.'

Fliss's lips tightened. 'I'll tell him,' she said, ushering Amy out of the door before she could change her mind about going. 'Um—see you later.'

It was an overcast morning and Fliss thought that it matched her mood. She was definitely not equipped to deal with Matt in her present state, and she hoped he'd understand why she'd brought Amy with her and back off.

To her surprise, the back door was locked, and, although she knocked a couple of times, no one came to open it. 'Is Matt still in bed?' asked Amy innocently, looking up at her mother with wide, enquiring eyes, but Fliss didn't know what to think.

'Let's try the other door,' she said, not wanting to commit herself, and they circled round to the front of the house, where they found Albert Freeman's van in the driveway and the front door standing open.

Fliss frowned. She'd known that the painter and decorator had given Matt estimates for the work he wanted done, but she hadn't realised an appointment to carry out the work had been agreed. Still, it was fairly obvious that it had, and she could only assume that that was why Matt hadn't opened the back door.

With Amy following close on her heels, she climbed the steps and entered the hall, immediately encountering a workman stripping paper from the walls. 'Oh, hi,' she said, when he caught sight of her. 'Is—is Mr Quinn about?'

'No,' began the man, but before he could offer any further explanation, Albert Freeman himself appeared from the back of the house.

'Oh, it's you,' he said when he saw Fliss, looking a little askance when he saw Amy beside her. 'Were you just knocking at the back door?'

Fliss warned herself to ignore his overbearing attitude, and said smoothly, 'I was looking for Mr Quinn. Do you know where he is?'

'London,' answered Freeman at once, and Fliss felt her stomach lurch in disbelief.

'London?'

'That's right.' Freeman was obviously enjoying being the bearer of unexpected news. 'He asked me to tell you that he won't need you this week. He'll be in touch when he gets back.'

Fliss hoped she didn't look as devastated as she felt. 'I see,' she said faintly as Amy tugged impatiently on her arm.

'Why has Matt gone to London?' she asked, voicing the question Fliss would have liked to ask herself, and the man gave the little girl a reproving look.

'That's none of your business, young lady,' he said, and Fliss suspected his words were meant for her as well. 'Now, you'll excuse me if I get on, won't you? Mr Quinn will expect me to have finished in the hall by the time he gets back.'

Fliss walked back to the cottage in a daze. She could hardly believe that Matt would take off for London without even having the courtesy to tell her where he was going. But then, after the way she'd behaved yesterday, he'd probably decided she didn't deserve an explanation.

But that was too simplistic. Matt wasn't like that. Whatever she'd done, whatever she'd said, she couldn't accept that he'd treat her so shabbily. Something must have happened, something that had required his immediate attention, and he'd left a message with Albert Freeman so that he could give it to her in person.

Well, that was one way of looking at it, she acknowledged, wondering if she was being simplistic now. He could have phoned her, he could have put a note through the cottage door. Surely he must have realised how she'd feel being ordered about by the tradesman. Albert Freeman had got great pleasure out of telling her she wasn't needed. Oh, God, what exactly had Matt said?

'Matt's gone to London.'

Amy announced the news to her grandfather as soon as she got through the cottage door, and Fliss saw her father's eyes widen in surprise as he lifted his head from the newspaper.

'London?' he echoed, much as she had done. 'And you didn't know he was going?'

'Obviously not,' said Fliss, realising that if she displayed anything but annoyance at the situation George Taylor would smell a rat. She shrugged. 'Perhaps it was an emergency.'

'And he couldn't ring you to tell you what he was doing?' Her father gave a disgruntled snort. 'I told you I didn't approve of you working for him. The man's totally thoughtless.'

Fliss forced a smile. 'I thought you said you'd changed your mind about him. Didn't you just ask me to tell him about some website before I left?'

'Huh.' Her father wasn't pleased to be reminded. 'Anyway, I should have known better. Men like him, they don't change. I bet he's gone sniffing after that Chesney girl again. Her father was telling me they'd had a bit of a bust-up. Apparently, she was totally opposed to him moving down here. I suppose it was only a matter of time before she persuaded him to change his mind.'

Fliss opened her mouth to tell him that if that was so, why was Albert Freeman decorating the hall and stairs? But she decided not to bother. For all she knew, Matt could be doing the house up to sell it again. Obviously, he didn't confide in her.

However, it was what her father had said about Diane that

troubled her the most. Despite his many statements to the contrary, deep inside she suspected Matt was still in love with the other woman. And now, thanks to Fliss's actions, he could resume his relationship with Diane, safe in the knowledge that his libido had been completely restored.

That hurt.

Even though she didn't believe he loved her, the possibility that he might be prepared to forgive Diane her indiscretions was painful. He'd been so adamant, so definite that Diane meant nothing to him. And yet, what else was she supposed to think when he hadn't even bothered to keep her informed of his movements?

It was all too much, and, excusing herself, Fliss hurried up the stairs to her room. She wasn't sorry for what she'd done, she told herself fiercely. Whatever happened, she would never regret being a part of his recovery. She just wished he could have chosen someone more worthy than Diane Chesney to love.

CHAPTER SIXTEEN

MATT drove back to Mallon's End in the late afternoon.

He had intended to get away straight after lunch, but Diane's arrival had delayed him. Her excuse, that she'd come to see his mother, had been convincing enough, but once they were outside the sickroom the real purpose of her visit had become clear.

'You can't really mean that you never want to see me again,' she protested tearfully, following him into his father's study instead of letting his mother's housekeeper show her out. 'All right. So I made a mistake. I'm not ashamed to admit it. But I don't love Tony. I love you, Matt. You can't blame me for turning to Tony when I thought I was never going to see you again.'

Matt looked up from the pile of mail that had accumulated during his mother's stay in hospital. It had only been a few days, but it was amazing how much junk had made its way through her letterbox. 'I don't blame you, Diane,' he said. However, he couldn't allow her to think that made any difference. 'I don't even blame Corbett for taking his chances.'

'Then—'

'I don't love you, Diane. I don't honestly think I ever did. I was flattered because you sought me out, that's all. It's not every day that a man's propositioned by a beautiful woman.'

Diane stared at him. 'So what's changed?'

'I have,' he said. 'It's as simple as that. I've decided I want more out of life than you can give me.'

'Like what?'

There was an edge to her voice now, and he knew she was having a hard time keeping her temper. 'Like a home, and children,' he answered her evenly. 'And you have to admit that that's something that's never interested you.'

'I could change.'

'But I don't want you to change,' he retorted mildly. 'Even if you were prepared to give up your life in London and move to Mallon's End, my answer would still be the same. I'm sorry but that's the way it is. What was it you said before? That I should move on? Well, I have.'

Diane's lips tightened. 'And I don't suppose your sudden desire to move on has anything to do with your new house-keeper, does it?' she snapped angrily.

Matt shrugged. 'Whether it does or not is nothing to do with you.'

'Your mother will never accept her!' she exclaimed scorn-fully. 'You should have heard her reaction when I told her Fliss had had a baby when she was sixteen. She was positively hor-rified.'

Matt tensed. 'Exactly when did you give her that piece of information?' he demanded. 'She's never said anything about it to me.'

'No, well, I suppose she couldn't,' Diane declared carelessly. 'I spoke to her on Tuesday evening. She rang me the day after she got back from Mallon's End. She was worried about you and Fliss Taylor. It must have been the next day that she had the stroke.'

Matt was stunned. 'You spoke to my mother on Tuesday evening?' he exclaimed savagely. And when she showed her assent, he wanted to choke her. 'You bitch,' he said. 'It didn't occur to you that whatever you said might have upset her? She had the stroke in the early hours of Wednesday morning, Diane. Just a few hours after you filled her ears with your jealous lies.'

'They were not lies.' But Diane was looking a little uneasy now. And typically for her, she tried to turn the blame back on him. 'I told her the truth, that's all,' she said defensively. 'If you hadn't wanted her to be upset, you shouldn't have got involved with someone like Fliss.'

'Someone like Fliss!' Matt was furious. 'You know nothing about Fliss, except what you've gleaned from gossip your mother's spread around. You shouldn't judge everyone by your own standards, Diane. Just because you'd sleep with any man who'd be fool enough to ask you, don't ever imagine Fliss would do the same.'

'Oh, I see.' Diane was spiteful now. 'She's turned you down, too, has she? Is that what all this sniping is about? Well, I could have told you you were wasting your time with frigid Miss Taylor. From what I hear, she must have had a virgin pregnancy.'

Matt was appalled by her comments. Appalled, too, that he could ever have thought she was the woman he wanted to spend the rest of his life with. He had no doubt that if Diane had had her way, the argument would have continued and become even more virulent. But Mrs Powell, his mother's housekeeper, had heard raised voices and came to warn them that they might be disturbing Mrs Quinn.

Matt had no hesitation then about asking Mrs Powell to show—or throw, if necessary—Miss Chesney out. And after she'd gone, he sat down at his father's desk and rested his head in his hands. Dear God, he was so tired of making stupid mistakes.

His mother had heard the raised voices, however, and a few minutes later Mrs Powell appeared again and asked if he would go up. Naturally she wanted an explanation, and Matt was relieved that the stroke that had had him driving madly through the early hours of Wednesday morning had apparently had no lasting effects. Her brain was as alert as ever, and, apart from a little residual numbness down her right side, she was expected to make a full recovery.

In consequence, Matt had no hesitation in assuring her that she should ignore anything Diane had said about Fliss. Yes, she had had a baby when she was sixteen, but that didn't make her a bad person. She'd made a mistake and she'd paid for it. But she was a good mother and she didn't have a reputation for sleeping around.

'So she has a child,' his mother said at last, and Matt found himself talking about Amy.

'She's a great kid,' he said. 'You'll love her, Ma, when you get to know her.'

'I am going to get to know her, then?' Mrs Quinn ventured drily, and Matt had had to admit that that was in the balance. Until he could see Fliss again, until he could speak to her, he didn't know what was happening. All he really knew was that he cared about her, deeply; that she'd helped him believe in himself again.

Now, as he neared the junction that would eventually lead to Mallon's End, Matt wished he could have spoken to Fliss herself. He'd had to leave a note pinned to the door for Albert Freeman. The tradesman had been due to start work the next day and Matt had left a key for him to find. He'd attached a note for him to give to Fliss, but he didn't know if she'd got it. Both times he'd phoned he'd got her father, and, despite the fact that he'd thought they'd ironed out their differences, George Taylor still gave off hostile vibrations.

Perhaps he should have confided in her father, told him the real reason he'd gone to London, but his experiences with the Press had left him chary of confiding in anyone. He didn't want to read about his mother's stroke in the next edition of the tabloids. She definitely wouldn't like it and he had to respect her privacy. Even if it meant suffering the pangs of anxiety for a few more days...

Fliss was in the front garden when the big Land Cruiser stopped at the gate. It was a warm, sunny evening, and she'd been thinning out some stocks that had become rank and over-grown. She got to her feet in some confusion when Matt pushed his way through the gate.

She hadn't known if she would see him again. Even though she'd told herself that he wouldn't waste money doing up the house if he had intended to sell it, the doubts remained. Her father seemed fairly convinced that they'd seen the back of him, but he had been acting antsy lately and she didn't know what was going on.

'Hi,' Matt said, allowing the gate to swing closed behind him. Then, almost awkwardly, 'You look busy.'

As an opening, it was as good as any, she supposed, tucking damp strands of hair back behind her ears. He could as easily have said hot, she reflected. She was hot, and sweaty, and definitely not prepared for their encounter however much she'd wanted to see him again.

Matt, meanwhile, looked good. No, better than good, she amended unwillingly. And so much better than he'd looked when she'd first seen him talking to Amy. He was dressed more formally than she was used to, his navy silk suit and pale blue shirt accentuating his cool elegance. He'd loosened his tie and the top button of his shirt, but that only added to his appeal. As always, he exuded a raw male sexuality that stirred emotions deep in her belly, and she acknowledged that he had proved far more dangerous to her peace of mind than she could ever have imagined.

Deciding to take her cue from him, Fliss smoothed the hem of the old cropped T-shirt she was wearing, wishing she'd taken Amy's advice and dumped the thing weeks ago. 'Um—have you just got back?'

'Just,' he agreed, taking off his jacket and hooking it over one shoulder. He waited until her nervous gaze connected with his again before adding, 'Did you miss me?'

Fliss's lips parted. 'I—I wondered how long you'd be gone,' she conceded carefully. 'Have—er—have you been to see Diane?'

A strange expression crossed his face. 'I've seen her, yes,' he said, and Fliss's stomach twisted into a tight knot of misery. 'Did you get my messages?'

'Messages?' Fliss put the emphasis on the fact that he'd said messages and not message as she'd expected. 'Mr Freeman told me you'd gone to London, if that's what you mean.'

'He *told* you?' Matt looked confused now. 'Didn't he give you my note?'

'A note?' Fliss wondered if she could believe him. 'No.'

'Dammit!' Matt shook his head. 'I wonder why the hell not. He was supposed to give you the note, not tell you what was in it.'

Fliss straightened her spine. 'Perhaps you didn't leave a note,' she said quietly. 'Perhaps you only thought you did. After all, you did leave rather unexpectedly, didn't you?' She paused, and then continued doggedly, 'I expect Diane was pleased to see you.' She swallowed. 'How is she?'

'Do you care?' Matt's expression had changed now, and, stepping over her gardening gloves and trowel, he came purposefully towards her. 'And I did leave a note.' His jaw compressed. 'What the hell is going on, Fliss? Are you glad to see me or not?'

Fliss backed up a little. 'I—well, how am I supposed to answer that?'

Matt scowled. 'It's not rocket science, Fliss. After the way you reacted the last time we were together, I think I have the right to ask the question.'

Fliss swallowed. 'Are you staying?' she asked tightly, and his scowl deepened.

'What kind of question is that?'

'Like you said, it's not rocket science,' she countered tartly. 'There's a rumour going round that you might be selling the house.'

'That's rubbish!'

Fliss's heart lifted a little. 'It's not true?'

'Of course it's not true.'

'But—Diane doesn't want to live in Mallon's End. You said so yourself.'

Matt stepped a little nearer, his breath a delightful coolness against her forehead. 'And that's where the rumour came from? The fact that Diane doesn't want to live in the country?' He put out a hand and touched her hot cheek. 'Are you sure you didn't start this particular rumour yourself?'

'No.' She was indignant, scrubbing her hand over the spot where his fingers had touched as if to erase it. Nor was she prepared to tell him it might have been her father. 'Does it matter who started it?'

'Not so long as you know it's not true,' he essayed drily. He looked down at her from beneath lowered lids. 'You know, I've tried to play this scene in my mind a dozen times on my way here, but it never turned out like this.'

Fliss backed up again. 'I'm sorry.' She licked her dry lips. 'But you went away without telling anyone what you were doing. In a village like this, people are always going to talk.'

Matt considered. 'And you didn't think about squashing the rumours?' he asked softly. 'You could have done.' He allowed his fingers to stroke a sensuous path from the frayed sleeve of her T-shirt to her wrist. 'You knew I'd be coming back.'

'Did I?' Fliss wondered if he realised how unlikely that sounded to her. 'You didn't confide in me either.'

'I wanted to.'

'Right.' She crossed her arms in an attempt at self-protection. 'So what stopped you?'

Matt sighed. 'Can we go inside? I'd prefer not to broadcast my private affairs to all and sundry.'

Fliss glanced about her. 'I don't see anyone, do you?'

'What's wrong?' Matt looked towards the cottage. 'Is your father at home? Has he warned you not to have anything more to do with me?'

'I'm not a child, Matt.'

'No, but I don't understand why you're so hostile. For pity's sake, it was an emergency, right? My mother was taken ill in the night. I didn't have a lot of time to do anything except write a couple of notes.'

Fliss stared at him, absorbing what he'd said with a wary reluctance. 'You—could have phoned,' she said at last, and he swore.

'I did phone,' he said harshly. 'Twice. Didn't your father tell you?'

'No. I—no.' Fliss stared up at him with troubled eyes. 'Are you sure? You actually spoke to Dad?'

'Gruff, clipped voice—one might also say hostile in his case, too? Yeah, that sounds like George Taylor to me.'

Fliss gasped. 'He never said a word.'

Matt nodded, gesturing towards the cottage again. 'All the more reason for me to speak to him now.'

'No—I—he's not here,' murmured Fliss unhappily, lifting her hands palms out in defence. 'He's taken Amy to the cineplex in Westerbury. There was a Disney film she wanted to see and he offered to take her.'

Matt's eyes darkened. 'Couldn't be better. We'll have plenty of time to talk.'

'Matt—'

'What?' His eyes dropped sensually to her mouth. 'We have to talk. You know that. After the way you brushed me off, I've gone through hell these past few days. Surely you're not going to deny me a few minutes of your time.'

Fliss moved her head from side to side. 'This—isn't a good time. I'm hot. I need a shower—'

'I'd say it was the perfect time,' he contradicted her huskily. 'Come on, Fliss, put me out of my misery. Tell me you're glad to see me.'

Fliss swallowed. 'I—whether I'm glad to see you or not isn't in question.'

'I'd say it was the only question,' he contradicted her swiftly. 'Well, are you? Would it please you to know that no woman has ever hurt me as much as you did?'

Fliss's jaw dropped. 'You don't mean that,' she protested, backing up the cottage steps behind her. 'Please, Matt, find someone else to make a fool of.'

Matt swore then, following her up the cottage steps. 'If anyone's the fool here, it's me,' he snapped, but, although his words were harsh, his eyes were dark with emotion. 'For God's sake, Fliss, I told you I loved you. Doesn't that mean anything to you?'

Fliss could hardly breathe. 'You—love—me?'

'That's what I said.' He glanced behind him and then stepped through the cottage door, swinging her round so that her back was to the wall behind her. 'You'd better believe it,' he added grimly and covered her mouth with his.

The unreality of what was happening gave way to a liquid hunger. His mouth was so intent, so insistent, a subtle exploration that reduced her limbs to water. She knew she must be making it easy for him, letting him see how utterly she succumbed to his demands. But right then, she didn't care. She'd missed him so much and she couldn't hide the way she felt.

'God, Fliss,' he muttered at last, resting his forehead against hers, 'you have no idea how you make me feel.'

Fliss drew a shivery breath. 'I think I do,' she whispered, lifting her hand and cupping his cheek. He hadn't shaved since that morning and already his dark stubble was rough against her fingers. 'But can we close the door before someone does come along?'

'Suits me,' said Matt unevenly, feeling behind him and pushing the door into its slot. Then, he put a hand at either side of her head and lowered himself against her. 'Now tell me why you didn't believe me when I said I loved you before.'

Fliss quivered. His lean body was hard against hers and she could feel his erection, hot and unmistakable, against her hip. 'Wh-what would you have thought?' she stammered, fighting the seductive pull of his mouth against her cheek. 'You—you'd just had sex—'

'Made love.'

'—for the first time in—in—'

'Almost two years,' he supplied helpfully, and she gave a convulsive sob.

'All right. In almost two years,' she agreed unsteadily. 'People say things in—in the throes of—of—'

'Passion?'

'All right. In the throes of passion,' she murmured, her face burning. 'They don't always mean them in the cold light of day.'

Matt's sigh was tangible against her earlobe. 'Fliss! Sweet, sweet Fliss! When I said I loved you I'd already recovered from any relief I'd experienced. I'd had a shower—a cold shower, as it happens. Coming downstairs and finding you waiting for me was—well, it was what I'd wanted all my life.'

'Matt—'

'No, I mean it.'

'But—well, it could have been Diane.'

For once he didn't react violently to her suggestion. 'No, it couldn't,' he said firmly. He drew back to look at her. 'Listen to me, sweetheart. To put it crudely, Diane tried to do what you did without any result. Any result whatsoever.'

'You mean—'

'She wanted us to have sex,' he said flatly. 'When I got back, naturally she expected us to carry on where we'd left off, but it wouldn't work. Whatever I'd felt for Diane before I went away was gone, vanished. I felt nothing when she touched me. Just a faint revulsion that I assumed was the way things were going to be from then on.'

'Then how—?'

Matt brushed her lips with his. 'Don't ask me how. I don't know. I just know that from the moment I met you, I started to come alive again. Not all at once, you understand, but slowly and surely. God, I couldn't believe how good I felt when you were around. I suppose that was when I started wanting you. Only I didn't believe that was going to happen either.'

'But it did,' she said, a dawning belief in what he was saying bringing a tender light to her eyes. 'Oh, Matt, are you really sure about this? We—we hardly know one another.'

'I know enough,' said Matt at once. 'I love you and I want to be with you. But if you need more time…'

'Don't be silly,' she said huskily. 'These past few days have been long enough for me, too.'

He kissed her again then, pinning her against the wall with his body, his hands moving possessively to cup her bottom and bring her more fully against him. The need to be with him was all-consuming, but Fliss pressed him back when he tried to unfasten her shorts.

'I—I do need a shower,' she protested, smiling at his

wounded expression. 'Come upstairs with me. You can wait in my bedroom, if you like.'

'And what if your father comes back?' he asked, following her up the stairs, but she only dimpled.

'He won't,' she said certainly. 'They'll be gone for ages yet.'

She was rinsing the soap from her body when the shower door opened and Matt stepped in beside her. He was naked and her jaw dropped in astonishment when he bestowed a hot, wet kiss on her open mouth. 'Let me,' he said, taking the bar of soap from the dish beside her, and, although she was almost finished, Fliss experienced the sensual delight of Matt's hands exploring every inch of her heated flesh.

He was heavily aroused and his erection kept bumping against her bottom. She longed to turn towards him, but once again he seduced her with his hands before satisfying her other needs. Then, encouraging her to wrap her legs about his waist, he lifted her onto him, and she felt again the satisfying thickness of him deep inside her.

'Now do you believe me?' he asked her hours later, when they were lying relaxed and replete on her bed. They'd made love again since that passionate interlude in the shower and Fliss buried her face in his shoulder, her lips moving against his warm flesh.

'I believe you,' she whispered huskily. 'I love you, too. So much. It frightens me.'

'What frightens you?' he asked, propping himself up on one elbow and looking down at her. 'You know I love you. I want to marry you, too, but I guess you need a little more time to come to terms with that.'

'Why?' She was curious.

'Well, you have Amy to think of,' he said gently. 'I wouldn't want her to think that I'm taking her mother away.'

'She wouldn't think that,' said Fliss surely. 'She thinks you're cool, you know that. My father, however, is another matter.'

'You think he won't approve?'

'He might be a little jealous,' she admitted ruefully. 'He used to be jealous of Amy's friendship with old Colonel Phillips, believe it or not. And he knows Amy likes you. She's never made any secret of the fact.'

Matt bent to caress one burgeoning nipple. 'Does this mean you will marry me, then?'

'Are you asking?'

'I'm asking.'

'Then I'll marry you.' She paused. 'Except—'

'Except what?' Matt stared at her.

'Why did you go to see Diane when you were in London?' she asked unwillingly. 'You never said.'

'Ah…' Matt gave her a wry smile. 'Well, I didn't go to see Diane. She came to see me. Well, ostensibly she came to see my mother, but that was just an excuse.'

'Oh, gosh, yes, your mother!' Fliss was horrified. 'I forgot to ask how she was.'

'Oh, she's improving,' said Matt easily. 'She had a slight stroke—'

'A stroke! So that was why—'

'I went dashing off to London in the middle of the night. Yeah.'

'And you told my father that?' Fliss was dismayed.

'No. I just told him to tell you I'd see you when I got back.' He grimaced. 'He didn't exactly encourage any further confidences, and I preferred not to discuss my mother's health with anyone else.'

'Particularly a newspaper reporter,' murmured Fliss drily, and he pulled a face.

'Am I that transparent?'

'Only to me,' she assured him softly. 'Oh, Matt, I do love you.' She paused. 'But is your mother all right? She's not going to be very happy when she finds out about us.'

'She already knows,' said Matt, surprising her. 'I told her how I felt about you. I took a chance that you felt the same.'

'Some chance,' said Fliss drily, and then heard the sound of a car pulling into the drive. 'Oh, lord, Dad and Amy are back. Are you ready?'

'As I'll ever be,' said Matt, bestowing one last, lingering kiss on her lips. 'Well, let's meet the in-laws, hmm?'

By the time Fliss had got her clothes on, the doctor was back behind his desk, and she emerged from the cubicle feeling rather flushed.

'Well, Fliss,' he said, as he'd said nearly eleven years before, 'my answer's positive. You are pregnant.'

Fliss caught her breath. 'I am?'

'I think you knew that,' said Dr Wheeler drily. He went to the door into the waiting room and opened it. 'You can come in now, Mr Quinn. Your wife's almost ready.'

Matt came into the room slowly with Amy dodging impatiently about behind him. His eyes went straight to Fliss's hot face. 'Hi,' he said. 'Are you—I mean—is everything OK?'

'As OK as it can be in her condition,' the doctor answered for her. He glanced at Amy. 'Does this young lady know about this?'

'Of course.' Matt spoke almost absently, his eyes still on his wife's face, and Fliss could tell that he badly wanted her reassurance.

'I'm three months pregnant,' she said, looking from him to Amy and back again. Then, turning to her daughter, 'You're going to have a baby brother or a baby sister.'

'Wow!' Amy was impressed. She had grown up a lot in the past year and having a father of her own had made all the difference to her. 'Kelly Mason is going to be *so* jealous!'

'Yes, well, we won't be telling anyone else for the time being,' said Fliss, linking her fingers with Matt's. She grimaced. 'At least until we tell your grandfather, anyway.'

George Taylor had begrudgingly offered them his blessing at last, and he had been somewhat mollified by the fact that his daughter was to be the mistress of the big house. Just across the churchyard, too, if he needed her.

'And your grandmother,' agreed Matt, nodding at his stepdaughter. 'You can tell her, if you like.'

'Coward,' said Fliss in an undertone, nudging his ribs, but

she didn't really mean it. In the three months since she and Matt had got married, Mrs Quinn had become a frequent visitor to the Old Coaching House. It was as if all she'd wanted was that her son should be happy, and there was no doubt in anyone's mind that he was. Plus, she and Amy had taken to one another from the start. The little girl had never known what it was like to have a grandmother. She'd been too young when Fliss's own mother had died.

Now the three of them left the doctor's surgery in Westerbury, and climbed into the Land Cruiser that was waiting outside. It was autumn, and the leaves on the trees were already turning to red and gold.

But the spring would be here soon enough, thought Fliss, resting her head on Matt's shoulder for a moment before he started the car. And with the spring would come new life, not just for the trees, but for her and Matt, too. And for Amy. She smiled up at her husband, thinking what a difference a year could make.

'Love you,' she said softly, and he squeezed her thigh.

'Love you, too,' he answered, and Amy poked her head between them.

'And I love you two as well,' she declared, and Fliss and Matt shared a smile of complete understanding as he reached to start the car.

Get *Sweet Revenge* from

PENNY JORDAN

this month and save money!

SAVE 50p

on *Sweet Revenge*
by Penny Jordan

Valid only until 31st June 2005

9 904170 570503

To the consumer: This coupon can be redeemed for £0.50 off *Sweet Revenge* by Penny Jordan at any retail store in the UK. Only one coupon can be used per purchase. Not valid for Reader Service™ books.

To the retailer: Harlequin Mills & Boon will redeem this coupon for £0.50 provided only that it has been used against the purchase of *Sweet Revenge* by Penny Jordan. Harlequin Mills & Boon reserve the right to refuse payment against misused coupons. Please submit coupons to NCH, Corby, Northants NN17 1NN.

SAVE 75c

on *Sweet Revenge*
by Penny Jordan

Valid only until 31st June 2005

9 823346 050758

To the consumer: This coupon can be redeemed for €0.75 off *Sweet Revenge* by Penny Jordan at any retail store in Eire. Only one coupon can be used per purchase. Not valid for Reader Service™ books.

To the retailer: Harlequin Mills & Boon will redeem this coupon for €0.75 provided only that it has been used against the purchase of *Sweet Revenge* by Penny Jordan. Harlequin Mills & Boon reserve the right to refuse payment against misused coupons. Please submit coupons to NCH, Corby, Northants NN17 1NN.

MILLS & BOON®

Live the emotion

Modern
romance™

POSSESSED BY THE SHEIKH by Penny Jordan

After being stranded in the desert, Katrina was rescued by
a Sheikh and taken back to his luxury camp. He decided to
marry her, though he thought her a whore. Then he
discovered – first hand – that she was a virgin...

THE DISOBEDIENT BRIDE by Helen Bianchin

Their marriage was perfect – and then billionaire Tyler
Benedict's wife left! Now he wants her back. Beautiful
Lianne Marshall can't refuse his deal – but this time she
won't play fair. However, Tyler is after more than a
business arrangement!

HIS PREGNANT MISTRESS by Carol Marinelli

Australian billionaire Ethan Carvelle left Mia Stewart years
ago. Now Mia's pregnant – claiming Ethan's late brother is
the father! Torn between duty and desire, he decides to
make her his mistress. But he knows nothing of the secret
Mia is hiding...

THE FUTURE KING'S BRIDE by Sharon Kendrick

Prince Gianferro Cacciatore is heir to the throne of
Mardivino and his father, the King, is dying. The pressure
is on Gianferro to find a wife and his heart is set on
English aristocrat Millie de Vere. But Millie hardly knows
the prince...

Don't miss out...

On sale 1st April 2005

*Available at most branches of WHSmith, Tesco, ASDA, Martins,
Borders, Eason, Sainsbury's and all good paperback bookshops.*

Visit www.millsandboon.co.uk

0305/01b

FREE!
4 Books
and a surprise gift!

We would like to take this opportunity to thank you for reading this Mills & Boon® book by offering you the chance to take FOUR more specially selected titles from the Modern Romance™ series absolutely FREE! We're also making this offer to introduce you to the benefits of the Reader Service™—

- ★ FREE home delivery
- ★ FREE gifts and competitions
- ★ FREE monthly Newsletter
- ★ Exclusive Reader Service offers
- ★ Books available before they're in the shops

Accepting these FREE books and gift places you under no obligation to buy, you may cancel at any time, even after receiving your free shipment. Simply complete your details below and return the entire page to the address below. You don't even need a stamp!

YES! Please send me 4 free Modern Romance books and a surprise gift. I understand that unless you hear from me, I will receive 6 superb new titles every month for just £2.75 each, postage and packing free. I am under no obligation to purchase any books and may cancel my subscription at any time. The free books and gift will be mine to keep in any case.

PSZEF

Ms/Mrs/Miss/Mr ....Initials...............................

BLOCK CAPITALS PLEASE

Surname ....

Address...

....

....Postcode ....

Send this whole page to:
UK: FREEPOST CN81, Croydon, CR9 3WZ

Offer valid in UK only and is not available to current Reader service subscribers to this series. Overseas and Eire please write for details. We reserve the right to refuse an application and applicants must be aged 18 years or over. Only one application per household. Terms and prices subject to change without notice. Offer expires 30th June 2005. As a result of this application, you may receive offers from Harlequin Mills & Boon and other carefully selected companies. If you would prefer not to share in this opportunity please write to The Data Manager, PO Box 676, Richmond, TW9 1WU.

Mills & Boon® is a registered trademark owned by Harlequin Mills & Boon Limited.
Modern Romance™ is being used as a trademark. The Reader Service™ is being used as a trademark.